Charlie felt his heart melt at Dana's four-year-old innocence

Her big blue eyes were irresistibly gorgeous. So this was how it would be to have your own child, your own flesh and blood, looking at you like you were Superman. At that moment he could slay a dragon for her.

He tilted her chin up and examined the damage. The cut wasn't very deep, and only about a centimeter long, but gaped in the middle. It had stopped bleeding.

"I reckon I can fix that good as new. Open your mouth, sweetie." Charlie smiled as Dana obeyed instantly, opening it as wide as it could go. Her neat white teeth all appeared to be intact, and he felt along her jaw up to the angle on both sides. "Well, I don't think you did any more damage."

He glanced up at Carrie to confirm it. She was looking at him with such an intense stare that he momentarily forgot about Dana sitting in front of him. He momentarily forgot to breathe.

Dear Reader,

I'm so happy you're reading Charlie and Carrie's story.

Dr. Charlie Wentworth is a real character—the black sheep of the family. He could have been a hot-shot surgeon. In fact, his family practically demanded it. But instead he chose a life of community medicine, challenging himself with a cash-strapped drop-in center for a poor, inner-city neighborhood.

Dr. Carrie Douglas is a dedicated bureaucrat pretending she'd rather push papers around a desk than put her medical degree to use. Scarred from an incident that all but ended her career, she's found a comfortable niche and is determined to climb the management ladder all the way to the top.

On paper they're a terrible match. One's a laid-back charmer, the other's an uptight control freak. They've both been burned in previous relationships. Plus, Carrie has her four-year-old daughter, Dana, to protect, while Charlie's living with the threat of a potentially fatal disease. But when Carrie is sent to shut Charlie's center down, there are serious sparks!

So buckle up for the ride and enjoy!

Love,

Amy

FOUND: A FATHER FOR HER CHILD
Amy Andrews

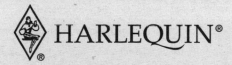

HARLEQUIN®

TORONTO • NEW YORK • LONDON
AMSTERDAM • PARIS • SYDNEY • HAMBURG
STOCKHOLM • ATHENS • TOKYO • MILAN • MADRID
PRAGUE • WARSAW • BUDAPEST • AUCKLAND

ISBN-13: 978-0-373-19902-0
ISBN-10:   0-373-19902-3

FOUND: A FATHER FOR HER CHILD

First North American Publication 2008

www.eHarlequin.com

Printed in U.S.A.

FOUND: A FATHER FOR HER CHILD

This book is dedicated to all those health care workers, agencies and volunteers who help with society's poor and disadvantaged. Thank you.

CHAPTER ONE

TWO more weeks. Two more weeks. Two more weeks. The words reverberated around Charlie Wentworth's head in time with the squeak in his back wheel. Two more weeks until he could start living again. The regular Sunday visit with his parents had left him with that familiar bitter taste in his mouth. Between his family's overt disapproval, the uncertainty over his health and tomorrow's invasion from the hospital administrator, he had a lot on his mind.

All he had to do was get through the next fortnight. Go through the motions. Co-operate with the hospital hatchet-wielder. See his patients. Take his meds. Keep focused. Go get the blood test. Wait for the results. Then he could get on with living.

Unless the test results were bad. Then what the hell was he going to do? He stepped on the accelerator out of pure frustration. He felt like his life had been on hold for years. The separation, the divorce and now this. The ancient Datsun strained and protested, gaining steadily on the car in front, and Charlie eased his foot off the pedal. Blowing the gearbox wouldn't bring the next fortnight to a close any faster.

Carrie Douglas flicked her gaze to the rear-view mirror and tensed as the car behind surged closer. Her headlights stabbed into the darkness and she prepared to dip her high beam. She could see Dana's blonde head slumped to one side, her cute face relaxed in a deep sleep, her ancient blanky snuggled against her cheek.

The other car fell back to a safe distance again and she relaxed. Driving at night on an unfamiliar road made her nervous. Carrying such precious cargo intensified the feeling. It was at times like these one realised that there was only so much as a mother you could do to protect your children. So much more was out of your control.

Thoughts about the job she was starting tomorrow turned over and over in her mind. The hospital was sending her in to sort out the financial mess of one of their inner-city outreach programmes. As far as projects went it looked pretty tedious but with her business and medical degree, she was perfect for the job.

And it wouldn't be long now until her hard work paid dividends. There were rumours she was being considered for promotion to department head. Both Anaesthetics and Paediatrics were coming up for renewal. From there it would be an easy springboard into the real management hierarchy. In five years she was hoping to make Deputy Medical Director. Glass ceiling be damned!

It was the only thing in her life that mattered other than Dana. She needed financial security for her daughter and herself and to show everyone that her unplanned career diversion had been successful. Losing sight of her goal was not an option. She'd even left her sister's wedding before the bride and groom so she could catch a decent eight hours' sleep to ensure she was in good condition for tomorrow's job.

Carrie saw the headlights of an approaching car illuminate the horizon and adjusted her headlights in preparation. She chewed at her bottom lip, going over everything in her head as the approaching car grew bigger. She glanced in the rear-view mirror again. The car behind was keeping a respectful distance.

* * *

Charlie was pulled out of his brooding thoughts in an instant as he noticed the drift of the oncoming car into the path of the car in front of him. *Into his path.* He became instantly alert, braking reflexively and at the same time noticing the brake lights of the car in front. Great, just the way his luck was running!

He swore as the car crossed the middle line, putting it on a collision course with the car in front.

Letting out an expletive, Carrie stomped on the brake pedal as the fancy red vehicle bore down on her. Her entire life flashed before her eyes. For a split second the world stopped. Her heart beat so loudly in her ears that nothing else registered. It pounded so frantically in her chest her whole body shook with its agitated rhythm. And then panic and instinct took over and she pulled hard on the steering-wheel. *Please, God, don't take me away from Dana.*

Carrie held her breath as the red car passed in a blur. For a split second she thought she was safe. But then the red car clipped the rear of hers and she felt her head snap forward, her seatbelt snap tight and her head fling back again, slamming into her headrest as her vehicle spun wildly round and round in the centre of the road.

Charlie swore again as the red car's trajectory changed on contact with the car in front.

It flipped, rising up over his Datsun, narrowly missing him. He looked in his rear-view mirror as it made contact with the road behind him, smashing into the bitumen and rolling several more times before coming to rest on its wheels in a mass of mangled metal and shattered glass. The remaining headlight shone brokenly on the unmoving form lying in the middle of the road.

* * *

'Dana,' Carrie called, turning frantically, ignoring the pain in her neck as they came to a stop in the middle of the road. Her daughter's eyes fluttered open briefly and then she stuck her thumb in her mouth and stroked her blanky against her cheek. Carrie's mother had always said Dana could sleep through an explosion.

Carrie felt a surge of relief so intense she almost floated out of the car. Dana was fine. Dana was fine. Her baby was fine. *Thank you. Thank you. Thank you.* Carrie felt an overwhelming urge to sink to her knees on the road and kiss the ground. She laid her forehead against the steering-wheel and took some deep calming breaths, the immediate shock giving away to the euphoric feeling of having just dodged a bullet.

It took a few seconds for the doctor in Charlie to respond to the inert form lying on the road, shock blunting his reactions. He opened his door, knowing he had to get to the victim lying on the road. But his eyes flicked to the other car that had come to a standstill in the centre of the road not far from him. The person inside was sitting at the steering-wheel, unmoving. Was this person also injured? *Two potential victims.*

The golden rule of triage—the most critical first. He looked back at the person on the road. Was he even alive? Could he have survived being flung out of a vehicle at high speed? He doubted it. He ran to the first vehicle and wrenched open the door.

'Are you OK?'

Carrie startled at the brisk demand coming back from the quagmire of her shock. Her heart was hammering like a runaway train, her hands still gripping the steering-wheel. Was she OK? She'd been too concerned with Dana to notice. Her neck hurt a little.

She blinked at the question. 'I'm f-fine.'

Charlie gave her a quick visual once-over. She didn't seem

to have any obvious injuries. He nodded. 'I have to go see to the other driver.' He indicated with his head.

Carrie nodded, noticing the very still person lying on the road for the first time. 'Yes,' she said.

And then the man was gone. She lifted her head, gingerly tested the range of movement of her neck. It was tender when she twisted it to the very limit of its capabilities but otherwise it seemed OK. Probably some minor whiplash. Still, Carrie knew how debilitating such an injury could be. She'd get an X-ray some time tomorrow to be sure.

Charlie popped the boot of his car and pulled out his medical kit, complete with oxygen and suction. In his line of work he needed a fully stocked kit ready to go in his car at a moment's notice, and tonight he was grateful that he'd decided to irritate his father and drive the Datsun. If he'd been driving the BMW, he'd have been up the creek without a paddle.

He sprinted to the inert form, his heart pounding, his pupils dilating as his brain processed all the possibilities. It was a man. A middle-aged man. Had he fallen asleep at the wheel or had there been a medical emergency like a heart attack or a stroke that had caused him to veer into their path?

Charlie donned a pair of gloves and assessed the man methodically as drilled into him during his student years. D. R. A. B. C. H. Danger. Response. Airway. Breathing. Circulation. Haemorrhage.

The man was unresponsive. Unconscious. His airway was compromised, his gurgling respirations concerning. He was breathing. Just. He had a pulse. But it was rapid and weak.

His face was covered in blood. Charlie looked at the car and noticed the massive hole in the windscreen. The man must have been catapulted out through the glass, sustaining numerous lacerations. A quick head-to-toe check revealed multiple contusions, bilateral fractured tibias and what appeared to be an arterial bleed from the femoral artery if the bright, pulsing blood from the man's groin was any indication.

Great! He tore the fabric of the man's jeans, pulled a wad of gauze out of his kit and placed it over the bleeding site, applying firm, even pressure. He needed help. He flipped open his phone and dialed triple zero with one hand and prayed for service in an area that was generally sketchy at best. The nearest ambulance was twenty minutes away.

'Hey, lady, I could use a hand here,' he shouted into the stillness of the night while he waited for the operator.

Carrie jumped, snapped out of her daze by the urgency of his voice. Of course. She was a doctor, for goodness' sake. But the thought of getting out of the car, of assisting the stranger, paralysed her with fear. The familiar dread descended on her and her heart was hammering madly again. He didn't know what he was asking. And anyway…she couldn't leave Dana.

Carrie watched him working as he spoke into the phone as if she was watching it on a television screen. Like it wasn't really happening. He obviously had a medical background. He was calm and capable, with a huge boxful of medical supplies at his side.

She had a strange feeling of disconnectedness. Maybe it was the residual effects of shock. Maybe his appeal for help had tipped her over. Her hands shook as she thought about getting out of the car and lending a hand. She couldn't do it. The mere thought was enough to make her hyperventilate. It terrified her more than the near collision had.

Charlie cursed as he hung up. They were coming, sending two road units and a chopper and alerting the nearby local rural fire brigade, but would it be soon enough? The man's obstructive breathing sounded loud in the night filled otherwise only by insect song. Hell! The driver needed his airway managed as well as his haemorrhage, and he couldn't do both.

'Lady! Get your butt here now,' he shouted, turning his head so he could pierce her with a look that was a cross between commanding and desperate. 'I'm trying to save this guy's life!'

Carrie felt the man's demand slice through her panic and touch the doctor she had shut away for too many years. Despite her shaking, despite the dryness of her mouth and the pounding of her heart, something inside responded to the stranger's urgent appeal. She checked on Dana. Still asleep. Almost against her will her hand reached for the door.

Charlie looked up as the woman approached. *Oh, hell.* She was pale and visibly shaking, looking at the unconscious bleeding patient as if she'd never seen blood before. She looked horrified, as if she was going to either faint or vomit. Or both. *Great.* She was going to be as useless as a screen door on a submarine.

She's all you've got, Charlie boy.

'Gloves top drawer of the kit,' he barked. If she didn't snap out of this stupor they were both in trouble. Yes, she'd been through a lot tonight. No doubt she'd thought she'd been a goner at one stage but there was a life hanging in the balance and time was of the essence. He didn't have time to baby her. He only hoped she would respond automatically to his demands.

Carrie crouched and pulled out a pair of gloves. Her movements were stiff, robotic, as if someone else was controlling her. Pushing her buttons.

'Down here. I need you to put your hand here,' he said. She didn't move and he almost lost it.

'I...c-can't.' Carrie's teeth chattered violently.

Charlie bit his tongue and took a deep calming breath. 'Look, lady, I know you've had a shock tonight but this is really, really important.'

Carrie felt herself responding to the softness in his voice. To his calm appeal. 'I c-can't.'

'Yes, you can,' he said encouragingly. 'I need firm, even pressure.'

His kept his voice quiet and composed despite the well of frustration rising inside him. Of all the people in the entire world he was stuck with a neurotic female who would probably faint before much longer.

He looked at her for confirmation and breathed a sigh of relief as she reached out a shaking hand to cover his. He removed his slowly. 'Firm. Even. Do you understand?'

She didn't answer him, just stared with a look of horror at the blood covering her glove. She was looking at it as if she'd never seen the substance before.

'Y-yes,' she stuttered.

Charlie looked down at her technique, pleasantly surprised to find that she had quickly mastered it. As long as she kept the pressure applied she could prevent this man from bleeding to death, and it freed him up to manage the airway.

Carrie didn't feel the bite of the bitumen into her knees through the thin fabric of her hand-made cotton tie-dyed trousers. She didn't hear the hum of insects or the stutter of her own panicked breath. She didn't even hear the stranger rooting around in his medical kit. The injured man's blood totally consumed her.

She could feel its warmth though the thin barrier of latex. She could smell its pungent metallic aroma heavy on the warm night air. Knew that it would be sticky as it clotted around her hands. *Don't die. Don't die. Don't die.* The chant helped her keep her mind off the roar of her own blood in her ears, the sweat beading her forehead, the nausea rolling through her intestines. She was breathing fast. Too fast.

Charlie cursed under his breath as he applied an oxygen mask to the man's face. She was going to hyperventilate at any moment.

'Hey,' he said, forcing himself to minister to her needs for a few seconds while the patient's life hung in the balance. 'You're doing great, OK? Just slow your breathing down. Can you do that?'

Carrie shook her head, feeling everything around her spinning out of control. Her lips were tingling. Her gloved fingers, covered in blood, were tingling. 'I can't…b-breathe,' she gasped.

Charlie bit back an expletive. 'Yes, you can. Look at me.'

Carrie couldn't move. She could only see the blood. Her mind started to play tricks. She was getting flashes of another place and time. Another patient. Another life-and-death situation. *So much blood.* She squeezed her eyes shut and shook her head to expel them.

'Look at me!'

His command ricocheted across the space between them and Carrie's head snapped up.

He saw the sheer panic in her eyes. 'You're doing really well,' he said gently, lifting his hand and squeezing her shoulder. 'The ambulance should be here soon.'

Carrie felt the warmth of his hand anchoring her in the suddenly spinning world and her panicked thoughts eased momentarily.

'What's your name?' he asked.

'C-Carrie,' she said.

'Hi, Carrie. I'm Charlie,' he replied, and smiled. 'I need you to slow your breathing down, OK? Do you think you can do that?'

Carrie nodded mutely.

'Come on, Carrie, like this,' he said, breathing deeply in and out himself. 'Breathe with me, like this.'

Carrie forced herself to slow her breathing. It was hard at first, she didn't feel like she was getting enough air into her oxygen-starved lungs. But following Charlie's calm voice, mimicking his deep steady breathing—in and out, in and out—

had an affect. His hand on her shoulder was immeasurably comforting. The tingling slowly subsided.

'OK, now. Good. This is good. Much better. Well done.'

He smiled encouragingly at her. Carrie was aware somewhere inside her jumbled thoughts that he was talking to her like she was a frightened child, the way she spoke to Dana during a thunderstorm. And she was also aware that behind his calm façade his eyes kept flicking down to check the inert man on the ground. Their patient was in bad shape and she had to pull herself together.

'I need to keep going here. Will you be OK? Just keep breathing, OK? In and out. All right?'

'I'm sorry. I'm g-good now. I'll breathe.'

Charlie searched her face. She still looked scared but the panic was gone. 'OK.' He nodded and turned his attention back to his patient.

What first? He needed a collar to stabilise the patient's neck before he manipulated it to improve the airway. He didn't have one. He made a mental note to put a collar in the kit for future use and moved to plan B. He knelt so that the patient's head was between his legs, his knees and thighs providing support for the head and neck.

He experimented with some gentle jaw support and chin extension and was relieved to hear the breathing become much less noisy. He reached for his portable suction unit, pushed the mask aside and placed the sucker inside the man's mouth. Blood slurped into the tubing.

Carrie startled at the loud mechanical noise. She saw the red fluid track down the tubing and looked away quickly. Nausea roiled through her intestines again and for an awful moment she thought she was going to vomit. Her heartbeat surged and she coughed on a rising surge of bile.

Charlie looked up quickly. 'You OK?' The look on her face was worrying. He could hear her fear in her tortured breathing as she struggled to get herself back under control. 'In and out, Carrie. This is nearly over.'

Carrie nodded, not trusting herself to speak.

Charlie felt his conscience prick at what this experience was doing to her. First she'd nearly lost her life and second he was forcing her to do something she was clearly unsuited to. She was obviously one of those squeamish people who didn't like the sight of blood, who flicked the channel over when a medical show came on television. It had to be hard for her. This sort of scene could be difficult for even hardened professionals.

She nodded, still not trusting herself to speak. 'Do…do you think he's going to d-die?'

Charlie was surprised to hear her talk. She looked mute with fear and her teeth were chattering loudly. Maybe she needed conversation to distract her from the grim reality of the situation? He had two choices. Truth or gloss.

'Probably.' He'd never much been one for gloss.

Carrie shut her eyes again.

'He's got a significant head injury and multiple fractures, including probable facial, which is compromising his airway. His pupils are fixed and dilated. He has a major arterial haemorrhage.'

Carrie nodded. Through the fog of her seized thought processes she knew these were significant, life-threatening injuries.

'But it's OK, I'm a doctor.' He grinned despite the circumstances, knowing she needed assurance. 'I'm not giving up yet.'

Carrie felt relief wash through her system. Maybe his confidence was wrong in the face of the severity of the situation but it helped calm her a little.

The wail of a distant siren interrupted their conversation. They both cocked their heads.

'See? Not much longer.' Charlie smiled.

A fire engine arrived a minute later. It wasn't quite what

Charlie was after but it meant more hands. 'What happened?' asked a thin young man, jumping out of the truck.

Charlie filled them in. Within a minute the car was being dealt with, a road block was being set up to manage any traffic and Charlie's request for light had been efficiently dealt with. He even commandeered someone to assist.

Second rule of triage—the most experienced person on scene managed the airway. But Charlie needed to get a line in and he couldn't do that from the head of the patient. He let one of the crew take his place, stressing the importance of neck stability while he quickly placed an IV in the crook of the patient's elbow. He hooked some fluid up to it and ran it wide open as another fireman held the bag aloft.

'She OK, Doc?' The human IV pole nudged Charlie.

Charlie looked down at Carrie, who had her eyes closed and was rocking her body slightly. *Not really.*

'She's fine,' he assured the fireman. The ambulance would be here soon and she could be relieved, but in the meantime she was doing a great job with the arterial bleed.

'OK?' he asked as he crouched down beside Carrie, squeezing her shoulder. She looked very pale. 'You're doing really well. I couldn't have done this without your help. I'm proud of you.'

Carrie looked at him, stunned by his praise. Amazed even more that it seemed to matter so much. She was a mess and she shouldn't have been. She should have been a professional. She could have been really useful. Formed a vibrant partnership to save the man's life. Been an asset instead of a liability. But he was complimenting her nonetheless and in this nightmare it really meant something.

Charlie contemplated splinting the man's fractured legs but discarded the idea instantly. He knew they'd probably want to put some special haemorrhage control trousers on the patient for his trip to hospital and splints would only hamper that process. He went back to managing the airway and keeping an eye on his unwilling assistant.

The road ambulances arrived five minutes later, one carrying an intensive-care paramedic, and the chopper thundered overhead minutes after that, landing on the road nearby. Carrie was relieved of her duty, her fingers numb from applying constant pressure. Someone took over and she felt several arms lifting her up and out of the way.

A paramedic shepherded her away but she refused to be looked at until she'd checked on Dana. Surely she wasn't still asleep? But she was. Soundly. Her cherubic pout slack, her blonde locks in disarray.

Carrie allowed the paramedic to give her a once-over by her car. Someone thrust a warm drink at her and someone else draped a blanket around her shoulders. She was grateful to be away from it all, her heart rate settling but the feeling of unreality persisting. Her neck ached and she rubbed each side absently. Her knees ached also. She looked down at her ruined trousers, torn and frayed at the knees.

She watched Charlie work in tandem with the paramedics to help stabilise the patient. She admired his confidence. His self-assuredness. She had practically fallen apart, almost vomited all over the patient. But not him. He had saved the man's life. His insistence that she help, while difficult beyond words for her, had been the right call. Not that she'd been capable of much.

Thirty minutes later the patient was gone. Dana finally woke up as the chopper lifted noisily. Carrie got her out of her car seat and snuggled her against her chest, wrapping the blanket around both of them.

'What happened, Mummy?'

'There was a car accident, sweetie.'

Dana yawned. 'It looks like a disco, Mummy. Can I dance?'

Carrie smiled. Dana was right. The scene did look like a

roadside discotheque. Flashing lights from the multiple emergency vehicles strobed across the scene, reflecting the pieces of broken glass scattered like diamonds across the road surface. 'No, sweetie, no dancing tonight.'

Dana gave her a cute sleepy smile and snuggled her face into Carrie's neck. Carrie hugged her closer, inhaling the sweet smell of her.

Charlie approached, surprised to see a mop of blonde hair peeking out of the top of the blanket. *She had a kid?* No wonder she'd been reluctant to get out the car.

'Is this your daughter?'

Carrie nodded.

'I'm sorry, I had no idea…' Maybe that's why she'd been so shaky? She'd probably still been reacting to the potential consequences had the red car hit hers head on.

'It doesn't matter,' she said. 'Dana slept through it all.'

'Who are you?' Dana's high voice broke into their conversation.

Charlie was captivated by a pair of big blue eyes fluttering behind heavy lids. 'I'm Charlie.' He grinned.

'Were you in the accident?' Dana asked sleepily.

'No, Sleeping Beauty, I just helped out.'

Dana giggled. 'Mummy, Charlie thinks I'm Sleeping Beauty.'

Carrie smiled down at her daughter. 'Go to sleep, then, Sleeping Beauty.' She dropped a kiss on Dana's forehead.

They both watched Dana drift off.

'How are you doing?' Charlie asked.

'I'm fine,' she assured him, despite the persisting tremble of her hands.

'I'm sorry, I was probably a bit forceful back there.'

'You were just trying to help him,' she said dismissively.

'You did well.' Charlie leant his hip against her vehicle.

Carrie laughed. 'Sure.'

'It's not everyone's cup of tea.' He shrugged.

Carrie decided it was best he didn't know about her qualifications. The chances that they'd ever meet in a professional capacity were fairly negligible. He was obviously an emergency medicine specialist and she was firmly ensconced in management.

'Are you going to be right to travel home?' he asked. 'Your car still goes?'

Carrie looked at the dented rear side panel. It did, but she doubted whether she could drive again tonight, she felt too shaken up. 'I'll get one of the tow-truck drivers to take it away and arrange to have it fixed first thing tomorrow. It's a bit of a pain but, considering I thought we were going to die tonight, it's an inconvenience I can live with.'

Charlie chuckled. 'You heading back to Brisbane? Can I give you a lift home?'

Carrie watched the traffic accident investigation squad put yellow markings on the road. They'd promised her a lift back into the city but they didn't look like they'd be finished any time soon.

She looked up into his face, taking notice of his looks for the first time. He was tall, a good head taller than her. He had nice eyes, grey eyes. A nice face, actually. Calm. Serene. Confident. Even when he'd been snapping orders he'd been completely self-assured. There was something innately tranquil about his features.

He had shaggy brown hair shot with blond, as if naturally streaked by the sun. It hung down, brushing his collar, and seemed to part naturally in the middle, falling in haphazard layers over his ears, just stopping short of impeding his vision. It was hardly inner-city chic, more 1970s rock star, but it suited his laid-back look.

Combined with his three-day growth, he looked a little hippy-ish and as far from Rupert's cleanly shaven short back and sides as was physically possible. His arms were tanned a deep brown, as if he'd spent a lot of time in the sun. His clothes were casual—threadbare jeans and one of those trendy T-shirts that looked like it had been painted by a preschooler. His chest was broad, his biceps firm in her peripheral vision.

'You can just drop us at the first taxi rank,' she suggested.

'Nonsense.' He rejected her suggestion. 'It's the least I can do for your help tonight. Where do you live?'

'Windsor.'

'Perfect. I live in the Valley. You're on my way.'

Charlie pushed away from the car. He cleared their departure with the scene controller while Carrie arranged for her car to be towed away.

Two minutes later he opened the passenger door to his sedan. Carrie eyed it disparagingly. The thought of leaving the scene with her precious cargo intact was amazingly lightening and for the first time since she'd met him, she could feel her old self returning.

'You sure this thing goes?'

Charlie feigned an insulted look. 'I'll have you know this is a classic car.'

'It's ancient.'

He chuckled. It was. It had been secondhand when he'd inherited it as his uni run-around. 'It's…retro.' He was fond of the old banger, preferring it to the ostentatious BMW his parents had bought him for his thirtieth birthday. It had lot of happy memories. He'd kissed his first girl in this car. Had driven to Ayers Rock in it. Slept in it the night of his bucks' party when he'd been too drunk to drive it home. The Beamer just didn't have the same amount of soul.

'Hmm,' she said, waiting for Charlie to position Dana's seat. 'We'll see how far it gets us.'

Dana stirred as Carrie buckled her into the seat. 'Where are we, Mummy?'

'In Charlie's car,' Carrie said quietly. 'He's taking us home.'

Dana looked around with heavy eyelids. 'I like it,' she murmured as her eyes drifted shut.

Carrie stood up and met Charlie's amused gaze. It was warm and sexy and she blinked, surprised by the parts of her body that were responding to it.

'Your daughter obviously has an eye for a classic.'

'She's four.'

His laughter followed her into the car and Carrie felt a warm sensation down low and deep spread out sensual tentacles until her whole body was humming. It was strange and unnerving and she put the brakes on immediately. So, he had a nice face and a great smile and had talked her down from the ledge tonight. She was a single mother with her eye on a prestigious job. She didn't have time for this.

Charlie started the car and they drove away slowly. It was a good minute before he lost sight of the multicoloured glow of the accident scene in his rear-view mirror. The adrenaline he had felt at the scene had dissipated, leaving him feeling edgy, and he drummed his fingers against the steering-wheel.

He took a sideways glance at his passenger. At least she was looking better than she had at the accident scene. There was colour in her cheeks now. She had auburn hair, he noticed for the first time. It was wavy rather than curly, tumbling to her shoulders and framing her oval face perfectly.

She had a creamy complexion with a smattering of freckles across her nose and big light brown eyes the exact shade of whiskey. She was wearing a purple tie-dyed shirt with a heavily beaded modest neckline and matching trousers. It was loose and flowing, hinting at her figure beneath rather than revealing it. She had exotic large silver hoop earrings and a thin silver choker with lines of purple beads hanging off it like icicles. The total effect was quite exotic. Very gypsy.

He adjusted the rear-view mirror so he could see Dana's

face. She was staring sleepily out the window, her blonde hair and blue eyes nothing like her mother's.

'So, what do you do?' Charlie asked, making small talk as the silence stretched between them.

Carrie felt her heartbeat pick up tempo. 'I'm…in management,' she said.

He laughed. She looked like she read palms for a living. 'Very vague.'

She shrugged. 'It's nothing very exciting. It pays the mortgage and the hours are good.'

He flicked a glance at Dana again. Her eyes had drifted shut. 'How old did you say Dana was?'

'She's four.'

'Cute age.'

Carrie smiled. 'Yes, it is. You got kids?'

Charlie snorted. 'No.'

OK, not into kids. 'Not your thing?'

Quite the opposite. Charlie had wanted a family of his own for a long time. A chance to do it better than his parents had. If that was possible. If he hadn't been genetically wired to screw it up as badly as they had.

He shrugged. 'Veronica, my ex-wife, didn't want them. It was probably just as well, given the divorce and everything.'

Carrie detected a bitterness scarring his deep voice. 'Was it bad?'

Charlie's knuckles grew white on the steering-wheel and Carrie wished she could have bitten her tongue off. She had no idea what had come over her. Maybe it was the moments they had shared at the accident scene that made her feel like she knew this man. That she could ask him such a personal question on such short acquaintance.

'Oh, God, sorry, that's none of my business. Forget I asked.'

He could hear the mortification in her voice and relaxed a little. 'It's OK. It was…kind of messy.'

They drove in silence for a little while longer.

'So, does Dana have a dad?'

Carrie shook her head, trying to keep her voice neutral. Unemotional. Even after five years Rupert's desertion still stung. 'Not one that's interested in her, no.' She looked out the window.

'Sorry.'

She shrugged. 'His loss.' Rupert had no idea what he was missing out on.

Charlie flicked another glance at the little blonde angel sleeping soundly in her seat. 'Absolutely,' he replied, his voice quiet.

She looked at him, hit by the sincerity of his tone. It was ridiculous to feel so connected to a person so quickly. She looked away and stared straight ahead. But his thigh was bulky and solid in her peripheral vision. His biceps flexed distractingly with every slight movement of the steering-wheel. He leaned forward and switched the radio on, his hair brushing against the neckline of his shirt and falling forward, momentarily obscuring the sexy stubble covering his jaw.

'Do you mind? Will it wake Dana?'

Carrie dragged her gaze away from his jaw. She laughed. 'She slept through a car smashing into us, four sirens and a helicopter.'

He chuckled. 'Good point.'

Charlie was grateful for the music to distract them from conversation. At the accident scene Carrie had been easy to dismiss as a blood-phobic, hyperventilating tie-dye flake. But seeing her now, free of the stress of the accident, she was a different woman altogether. One that appealed to him immensely. She had teased him about his car, sympathised over his divorce and told him about her little girl. Suddenly she was three-dimensional. Complex.

Desirable even. The thought slid insidiously into his head.

No. No way. She was a single mother. You didn't mess with them. Honourable men knew that. Especially not when his life was such a mess. A separation, a divorce and an almost year-long health crisis. In two weeks he'd have some closure, but until then his life was on hold.

And after that? There were things to do. Big things. A major project that had been shelved for too long was a priority. He wouldn't have time for an exotic single mother and her cute child. Relationships were going to be light from now on. Nothing heavy. His life had weighed a tonne for years. And women with children deserved more than that.

They passed the rest of the trip listening to the music and indulging in occasional light conversation. Charlie was grateful when he pulled up outside her apartment block. Her laughter and her scent had filled the car. He couldn't hear the squeak of the back tyre any more or smell the slight aroma of rust. And he liked those things about his car. OK, it was probably a guy thing—heaven knew, Veronica had hated every inch of it—but he liked them a lot. And it was disturbing to think this woman could completely obliterate them.

'Thanks for the lift, Charlie. And for…you know… snapping me out of it back there.' Now she was home she didn't want to get out. Strangely she felt like staying in the car, chatting with him. They'd shared an experience tonight that few strangers shared. They'd saved a man's life. She felt a weird kind of connection.

'Thank *you*,' he said. 'I know that wasn't easy for you. You did good. Really.' Charlie wanted her to go as desperately as he wanted her to stay. It was an unsettling feeling. It was as if they'd developed a strange kind of bond. 'I'll help you with Dana.'

They got out of the car and Carrie ducked her head to unbuckle Dana. She managed to pick her up without disturbing her.

'I'll get the seat,' Charlie said.

Being unfamiliar with children's safety seats, he made a real hash of it. 'How do you get the blasted thing out?'

Carrie laughed. 'Here.' She gently passed Dana to him. 'Move aside I'll do it.'

Charlie felt a funny tightening in his chest as Dana murmured and wriggled in his arms, trying to find the most comfortable position. Her blonde head snuggled into his neck and her hair smelt like toffee-apples.

Carrie removed the seat easily and he indicated for her to precede him. Carrie placed the seat on the ground and opened the front door. She turned and held her arms out for Dana. Charlie passed her over gently.

It was such a domestic scene Charlie couldn't quite believe he was in it. Or how…nice it felt. It had an odd kind of pull. But his life was complicated, his head was messed up and she had a child. And he'd probably never see her ever again. They were hardly compatible.

'Well, thanks for this, Charlie. I really appreciate it. It was nice meeting you. I just wish it had been under different circumstances.'

He chuckled. 'Amen to that.'

Carrie walked through the door and closed it without looking back. She put Dana to bed, trying not to think about the sense of intimacy she'd had when Charlie had handed Dana back. It was insane to think that way. Charlie was gone. The book had shut on their brief encounter. She had a daughter to raise and a career to forge.

She didn't need any Charlies in her life.

CHAPTER TWO

CHARLIE sat at his desk on Monday morning and drummed his fingers impatiently. He'd slept badly and his first appointment was late. He was annoyed. Just because he ran a drop-in centre, it didn't mean he had time to wait around for nosy hospital administrators.

He picked up the phone and dialled Joe's number. His best friend answered with his usual jovial greeting.

'Deep, philosophical question for you. Is it insane to fantasise about a woman who nearly vomited over you and you had to talk out of a panic attack?'

'And this couldn't wait half an hour?'

'Nope.'

'Is she hot?'

'Hell, Joe, I said deep.' Charlie laughed. 'We saved a life together. Well…actually, she was a mess but…I can't stop thinking about her.'

'OK, buddy, back up. Tell me the story.'

Charlie relayed the details of the previous night's incident. 'She's so not my type. She looked like a gypsy. She was wearing tie-dye, for God's sake. You know I prefer pinstripes.'

'Like vile Veronica?'

'Well…yes.'

'Oh, yeah, that turned out so well.'

'Well, it should have.'

'Your ex-wife was a stuck-up cow. Strikes me you could do with a little tie-dye.'

'She has a child. A little girl.'

'OK, stop right there.'

'I know, I know. It's crazy. I shouldn't be thinking like this.'

Joe laughed. 'Relax, Charlie. It's just the celibacy talking, man. In two weeks' time the tests will come back negative and you can get back on the horse. No man can think straight after a year of no sex.'

Charlie nodded. His friend made a very good point. 'Right.'

'Right. So…see you soon?'

'Right.'

Charlie hung up the phone and checked his watch, his thoughts returning once again to Carrie. *Damn it!* He drummed his fingers more loudly.

Carrie was late. It was unprofessional and rude. She tried the number again but was blocked by yet another busy signal. Last night's accident had sure thrown a spanner into the works. Having to arrange insurance and quotes and organise a hire car this morning had not been conducive to punctuality. And she'd slept badly, tossing and turning and thinking about Charlie all night.

She stood in front of the drab-looking building that she'd been assigned to and felt uncharacteristically depressed. A faded sign on the front announced it was the Valley Drop-In Centre. *God, I'm tired.* She pushed through the mesh reinforced glass doors and looked around the room.

'Dr Wentworth?' she asked a couple of bored, tatty-looking teenagers. They pointed to a closed door and she approached it briskly. She had a job to do and regardless of her near-death experience last night, she needed to put it aside and concentrate on today. *Concentrate.* The chipped nameplate said

'Dr Charles Wentworth'. She thought of Charlie and then shook her head disgustedly. *Concentrate, damn it!*

She gave a brisk rap.

'Come in.'

Carrie took a deep breath, pushed the door open and walked into the office. She stopped in mid-stride, knowing instantly who the tall rangy man with the shaggy downcast head sitting behind the desk was and gave a startled gasp.

Charlie looked up at the noise, his pen stilling in surprise. 'Carrie?'

'Charlie?' A sinking feeling formed in the pit of her stomach. *He couldn't be.* 'You're Dr Charles Wentworth?' she asked, hoping desperately that he was just there doing some locum work for the good doctor who she'd assumed to be years older.

'The very same.' He nodded. Surely she wasn't his appointment? 'And you're…Dr Douglas?'

Carrie nodded, temporarily unable to form words.

Charlie stared in dismay at her smart businesslike suit. Navy blue. Rich, red, silky blouse. Pinstripes. No tie-dye in sight. *Pinstripes—hell!* 'And you're here to…'

She nodded again. 'Audit you.'

The wall clock ticked so loudly in the silence it might as well have been a bomb. Charlie recovered first, ignoring the ominous 'A' word and its implications to the viability of the centre. He'd lived under the cloud of closure since he'd opened the clinic five years ago.

'*You're* a doctor?' *What the hell?*

Carrie lifted her chin. She'd never had to justify her title before and she was damned if she'd do so now. For the next month she was in charge here so it was imperative that she assert her authority immediately. Having him think less of her qualifications, ones she'd worked long and hard for, ones her parents had worked two jobs and re-mortgaged the house for, rankled. 'Yes, I am.'

Charlie was flabbergasted. He couldn't have been more surprised than if she'd told him she was a hooker. 'A medical doctor?'

'Yes, Charlie, a medical doctor.'

'You could have fooled me.'

She shrugged, trying for nonchalant when in reality her heart was hammering madly in her chest. Surely he could hear it? 'I've been in management for a while now.'

'I thought only middle-aged has-beens went into management.'

No. Sometimes young has-beens did, too. 'It's a legitimate career option these days. I'm on track to become the youngest hospital MD in Australia.'

Whoa—real party girl. 'So, what, when other little girls wanted to be fairies and princesses, you decided to chose something more—' *boring* '—practical?'

Carrie felt her spine stiffen. She was used to subtle male putdowns. Making her way in a male-dominated career had given her a thick skin and a very low tolerance level for fools. Why did he make ambition seem so dirty? Would he have asked her the same question had she been a male? Where was the man from last night who had so tenderly handed Dana to her?

'Do powerful women threaten your masculinity, Charlie?'

OK. This conversation was bizarre. She was standing before him in her fashionable pinstriped suit—*hell, pinstripes—*that moulded curves he hadn't even been aware of last night. Her collar was up on her soft, wine red shirt very chic and it clung to the very interesting rise of flesh that strained against the buttons, barely succeeding in concealing her cleavage.

Indignation burned in her eyes behind trendy frameless glasses that sat high on her perfectly straight nose. She had some shiny gloss stuff on her full lips, the only make-up he could detect, and they glistened. Her wavy hair was pulled back, restricted in some kind of clasp thingy, not a stray hair in sight.

She was the epitome of a modern businesswoman. Composed. Professional. Collected. And a far cry from the cot case of last night. Pale. Shaken. Hyperventilating. Try as he may, he just couldn't reconcile the two images. It was as if last night hadn't even happened.

'Not at all,' he said dismissively. 'Actually, I find powerful women very sexy. Hell, I even married one. I just couldn't think of anything worse if I tried. Management.' He shuddered. 'All that paperwork.'

Carrie swallowed. *Did he find her sexy?* The idea was as seductive as it was preposterous. She reeled in her straying thoughts. What the hell did she care if he did or not? Whatever happened to asserting her authority? She was going to need to be twice as hard with this man now he'd already had her at a disadvantage. Now he'd seen her so vulnerable.

'Yes,' she said briskly, bringing the conversation back to the matter at hand. 'Apparently paperwork's not your forte.'

Charlie chuckled. Paperwork was the bane of his life.

Carrie pursed her lips disapprovingly. He could find this as amusing as he liked but it was just irresponsible as far as she was concerned. When you were running a business, particularly with someone else's money, you had to be fiscally accountable.

'It's taken me a while to decipher some of your figures, particularly the last year's, and a lot of it's incomplete. To finish my investigation I'll need to see all your business files, bank records, activity statements and so on.'

Charlie stared at her, his ire rising. She was looking so prim and proper. So together. So unlike the woman from last night. She held the upper hand and she knew it. The future of the clinic depended on the outcome of her report. 'I have some of them ready. I'll have to get the rest together for you,' he stonewalled.

Carrie heard the flint in his voice. She glared at him. Did he think because he had already seen her at less than her best that she was just going to fold and meekly surrender? He needed to know now that the woman he'd seen last night had been a complete anomaly.

'You've had over a week to get this information together,' she growled, trying to keep her temper in check. 'I don't appreciate these stalling tactics.'

Tactics? 'Lady, what the hell is it you think we do here all day? I don't have time to scratch myself most of the time. Trying to locate five years' worth of documentation with the few snatched minutes that I get isn't possible. You know, I'm trying to practise a little thing called medicine here. Not that I expect *you* to understand that.'

Carrie felt the barb hit her in the chest and put her hand on her hip to steady herself from the impact. She'd wanted to be a doctor ever since she'd been able to say the word. Being judged by him professionally and found to be lacking was a new experience for her. Especially when he was basing his assessment on last night's performance. That was hardly fair. It had been four years since she'd had a clinical role. Her management skills, on the other hand, were very highly praised. It was like comparing apples and oranges.

'Please, don't call me lady. Doctor or Carrie will be fine.' The frost in her voice could have frozen a lake.

'I guess it'll have to be Carrie, then.' *If she wanted to be called Doctor she was going to have to earn it!*

She got his meaning loud and clear. And ignored it. 'I'll start with what you've got,' she said haughtily. 'How about you show me around, allocate me an office and I'll get started?'

Charlie gave a harsh laugh. He couldn't believe he'd lain awake all night thinking about this woman. Did she have any idea what it was like at the coal face any more?

'This isn't some posh city specialist clinic, Carrie. We

don't have offices to spare. There's only mine and the one opposite.' He pointed to the door behind her across the hallway and watched the line of her neck and the interesting pull of fabric across her chest as she twisted to check it out.

'It's used most days by our regular clinic holders so you'll have to vacate it during those times. Other than that there's the staffroom.'

Carrie glared at him. How was she supposed to work being shifted from pillar to post all the time? 'I need somewhere without constant interruptions.'

Charlie almost smiled at her, half expecting her to stamp her foot. She was annoyed? Good, she was bugging the hell out of him. She didn't look so prim and proper any more, he noted with satisfaction. So untouchable. She looked ruffled. Like she wanted to swear.

Her chest rose and fell a little faster, straining the button holding everything together. Her teeth bit into the soft fullness of her lower lip. She looked a little frazzled. A little like last night. She looked touchable. Very touchable.

He shrugged. 'They're your choices.'

Some choice. 'Which one will have the fewest interruptions?'

He snorted. 'Ever heard of the chaos theory?'

Carrie gripped the handle of her briefcase tighter. 'Gee, no, I must have been off painting my nails or polishing my tiara the days we discussed that in physics.'

He laughed despite his exasperation. 'All right, OK, sorry. Well, forget it. This place is chaotic and, trust me, there is no underlying order.'

Carrie waited patiently, hand still on hip, barely resisting the urge to tap her foot. She quirked an eyebrow at him.

Charlie sighed. Whether he liked it or not, he was stuck with her. 'The staffroom's your best bet.' He rose to his feet. 'Follow me. I'll show you around.'

Carrie stood aside as Charlie brushed past her. She caught a faint whiff of his aftershave and fought the urge to hurry, to keep pace with his long-legged stride. Every sensible cell in her body was telling her to her distance. And she was listening.

He was dressed as casually as he'd been last night. Trendy ultra-long shorts that fell just past his knees and another pre-school-inspired T-shirt. Since when had a man's clothes been so fascinating?

He took her out to the front area first. 'This is the reception area.' Charlie checked his watch. 'Angela should be in soon.'

'Angela?'

'She's the receptionist.'

'Why isn't she here already?'

'She's a local divorced grandmother who cares for her two grandkids on a permanent basis. She arrives after she's dropped them at school.'

'Surely it would be more efficient to have someone here when the clinic first opens?'

Charlie looked down at her. He could see her business brain already writing recommendations. 'Angela is invaluable. As a single mother yourself, surely you can see the advantage of being flexible?'

Carrie was torn between the emotional answer and the fiscally responsible answer. She gave herself a mental shake. She wasn't paid to think emotionally. 'Flexible isn't always good for the bottom line.'

Hell, he despised bottom-line thinking. There was no room for people in bottom-line thinking. 'Wait till you meet her. You'll understand.'

He moved over towards the games area, not wanting to get into a fruitless discussion with a bottom-liner over their obviously different visions. 'As you can see, we have a ping-pong table and a pool table, a small library, a lounge area and a jukebox.'

Carrie nodded, picking up a ball off the pool table as she

watched the two teenagers she'd seen earlier battling it out at ping-pong. 'The purpose of these being?'

He eyeballed her. Did he have to explain it? 'Recreation.'

'Is it a medical centre's role to provide recreation?'

Bottom line again? 'This is a drop-in centre, Carrie. It's not just about fixing people's ailments. A large portion of our client base is homeless kids, disaffected youth. If they're in here, listening to music or shooting pool, then they're not out on the streets, shooting drugs.'

Drugs? 'Shouldn't they be at school?'

Charlie snorted. 'Of course they should but guess what? Telling them they should be at school generally doesn't work—their parents have already tried that. Look, we get a lot of community support groups come through the centre every day, talking to the kids that are around, helping them to get their lives together. We can't do that in a sterile judgmental environment. These are kids who have huge trust issues. We have to provide an environment where they don't feel judged, where they feel comfortable, where they feel safe. In fact, if I had my way, we'd be expanding the services we offer here. This area is crying out for a properly resourced centre.'

Carrie replaced the pool ball and pondered his statement for a moment. She felt a needle of guilt prick her conscience. He was doing what she'd wanted to do in the beginning. The reason she'd become a doctor in the first place. To help people who couldn't afford the luxuries that a lot of people took for granted. Like health care. Having grown up poor, she'd always wanted to give something back. Then a child had died because of her negligence and everything had changed. Practising medicine had no longer been an option.

Charlie watched her wander around the lounge area, absently touching furniture, caressing books. *Pinstripes?* Damn it, this was his fault. He'd been sent the usual 'please give reason' letter by the hospital board two months ago. He should have just sent the standard reply, heavy on politics and designed to guilt the suits into backing down.

But this time, with all the uncertainty in his life this past year, he'd been indignant and defiant. He'd not only been scathing of their continual attacks but suggested that they leave him the hell alone to do what he did best.

Watching Carrie's bottom sway in her pinstriped skirt as she ran her fingers over the jukebox buttons, he wished he hadn't. His recalcitrance had, no doubt, earned him this surprise audit. In short, he had brought this intrusion on himself. Had brought Carrie and her pinstripes on himself.

'We have a small treatment room,' he said, and turned to show her the way. He opened the door, hyper-aware that she was right behind him. 'I do a lot of stitching up in here.'

Carrie looked at the scrupulously clean white room. The rest of the centre was a bit on the dowdy side. The walls were marked, the furniture had seen better days, the lino flooring was scuffed and worn in places. But this room could have done a hospital proud. From the military neatness of the made-up examination bed to the crisp antiseptic smell, it was a credit to the clinic.

'Wow.'

Charlie chuckled. 'This is Angela's baby. She's an ex-army nurse. Vietnam.'

'Do I hear somebody talking about me?'

'No ma'am.' Charlie winked at Carrie. 'Not me.'

Carrie dragged her gaze away from Charlie's face and her mind off the unexpected tightening of her stomach muscles to look at the older woman. She was tall and built like a female Olympic hammer-thrower, with an ample bosom, greying hair and shrewd, assessing eyes. She looked like someone not to be messed with.

'Angela, this is Carrie.'

Angela sniffed. 'The suit?'

Charlie smiled at his ever-loyal receptionist. 'The suit,' he nodded gravely.

Carrie felt assessing eyes on her. 'Hey, I'm not the enemy here,' she protested.

'Hmph!' Angela grunted. 'We'll see.'

'OK, moving right along.' Charlie ushered Carrie down the hallway and opened the door. 'Here's the staffroom.' He strode over to a row of grey lockers in the corner. 'You can put your stuff in here.' He tossed her a key. 'Lock up any valuables. Some of the best petty thieves in Brisbane frequent this place.'

'Er, right.'

Carrie looked around the room. It was a little on the used-looking side, as well. The kitchen area had chipped benches, the kettle was ancient and the fridge had long since stopped being white. But it was a decent size with a big table in the middle that sat twelve—perfect for her laptop.

'Toilet through there.'

Carrie followed the direction of his pointing finger. He dropped his hand and strode towards a door in the back wall, which he opened.

'Basketball court out the back.'

'More recreation?'

Charlie laughed. 'More recreation. Every lunch-hour I'm on the court, trying desperately to outplay a bunch of kids twenty years younger than me.'

Really? 'And here I was thinking you didn't have time to scratch yourself.'

Charlie sobered. 'It's all about trust, Carrie. I need these kids to trust me.'

'And basketball achieves this?'

He shrugged. 'Basketball helps.'

The movement of his shoulders drew attention to his shirt. 'I suppose your workclothes do, too?'

'Not many kids around here respond favourably to someone in a suit.'

The hallway door opened abruptly. 'Hey, Charles, my man, only two more weeks and you're back in the game.'

Carrie blinked at the intrusion on their conversation. *Two more weeks? Back in what game?*

'Oh…sorry, didn't realise you had company.'

Charlie shut his eyes and wished this day was over. At least Joe had the grace to look embarrassed. 'Joe, this is Carrie.'

Carrie glared at him. He held up his hands. 'Dr Carrie Douglas.'

Joe's eyes lit up. 'Carrie. What a lovely name.' He stuck out his hand.

Charlie rolled his eyes. 'The hospital administrator I was telling you about.'

'Ah, the suit,' Joe said as he shook Carrie's hand.

Carrie laughed. She was getting the distinct feeling her arrival had been discussed at length. 'Apparently.'

Charlie was inordinately irritated by Carrie's response to his friend's flirting. Did Joe never turn off?

'Joe works at a posh city law practice but does some *pro bono* legal work for our clients. He's here most mornings.'

'And most lunch-hours.' Joe winked.

'That's very generous of you,' Carrie said.

Give me a break. 'He plays basketball at lunch,' Charlie said dryly.

'Well, no doubt I'll be seeing you around over the next few weeks,' Carrie said. She placed her briefcase on the table and opened it, removing her laptop. 'I guess I'd better get cracking. The sooner I get this done the sooner I can be out of your hair.'

They left her to it. Charlie was glad to shut the door on her and put some distance between them.

'Man, is she a hottie or what? You see those curves? Move over, Nigella.' Joe clapped his best friend on the back.

'She's a pain in the butt, that's what she is.'

Joe laughed. 'Relax, mate. They're never going to shut this place down. The outcry would be huge. No one has the guts.'

Charlie sat behind his desk and sighed. 'She's the woman from last night, Joe. The one I was telling you about.'

'The tie-dye chick?'

Charlie nodded miserably.

Joe stifled a grin. 'Pinstripes, huh?'

Charlie groaned and dropped his head down onto the table, banging his forehead a few times.

'She's a doctor?'

Charlie looked up from his desk. 'Apparently.'

'Hmm, intriguing, as well.'

'Pain in the butt,' Charlie said, sitting up, closing his eyes and letting his head fall back against the headrest as he idly swung the swivel chair back and forth, Joe's laughter all around him. He opened his eyes and looked at his friend. 'Shut the door on your way out.'

Joe laughed again and departed.

Hours later Carrie was deep in figures when the door opened and a group of noisy, grungy-looking teenagers trooped through the room, eyed her suspiciously and continued to the back door and out to the basketball court. Joe winked on his way past.

'Wanna shoot some hoops?'

Carrie looked down at her unsuitable clothes. And her stilettos. 'Ah, thanks, better not stop.'

Charlie came through moments later. He acknowledged her with a quick nod of his head.

'How are we looking?' He opened his locker, reached for his medication bottles and took one tablet from each.

Carrie took off her glasses and rubbed her eyes, opening them to find him dishing out tablets. She watched him go to the sink, pour a glass of water, put the tablets in his mouth and drink the entire contents of the glass. 'Too early to tell,' she said, her curiosity well and truly piqued. *Were they vitamins?* He looked like he took care of himself. 'It'll take me a fortnight at least to wade through everything.'

Two weeks? Hell! He had to put up with her pinstriped suits for a fortnight? As Joe kept reminding him, he only had fourteen days to go on his enforced celibacy—and she was going to be here for every one of them? 'That long?'

She nodded. 'I've been allocated a month.'

A month!

'It'll be faster if I get that paperwork sooner rather than later.'

'I'll have it on your desk by the morning,' Charlie said as he departed to join the others. Even if he had to stay all night.

Carrie switched her laptop off at five o'clock. She should make it home by five-thirty, in time to get Dana's tea. She felt a pang of regret that she couldn't be home more for her little girl. But, like it or not, she was a single mother with no support from Dana's father. Susie, her live-in nanny, was a godsend. Dana adored her and Carrie had no idea what she'd do without her.

The ebb and flow of human traffic that had swirled around all day seemed to have diminished, she noticed as she walked down the hallway. The jukebox was now silent and she realised as she quietly hummed a song that it had been played so often it had worked its way into her subconscious.

'I'm off,' she said, stopping at Charlie's open door out of courtesy.

'Good for you. I'll be here all night, getting that paperwork together.'

Did he want her to feel sorry for him? A job he'd had a week to do? 'That would be most helpful. Thank you.'

'Doc!'

The voice was so loud, so unexpected that Carrie visibly

startled. She turned to the source of the noise and watched a young man stride into the clinic, carrying another man like a sack of potatoes over one shoulder and a bawling toddler on the opposite hip.

Charlie was up and out of his chair and brushing past a still startled Carrie in a matter of seconds. 'What is it, Donny?' he asked, opening the door of the treatment room. 'He's not a regular. Do you know him?'

Donny nodded. 'His name's Rick. He uses smack. He had a needle hanging out of his arm when I found him.' Donny laid the unconscious man on the examination table.

'Carrie, take the baby,' Charlie said, raising his voice to be heard over the distressed child as he pulled on some gloves and placed an oxygen saturation probe on Rick's finger.

'Whose is it?' she asked. *Please, please, please, don't let this poor frightened child belong to the person lying still and cyanotic on the bed.*

'She's my niece,' Donny said, and handed her over gratefully, looking more at home with a nearly dead drug user than the pretty little girl with pink ribbons in her hair. 'I'd just taken her to the park when we came across him. I couldn't just leave him.'

Carrie automatically rocked the child. 'What's her name?'

'Tilly.'

'It's OK, Tilly, you're safe now, it's OK,' Carrie whispered, cradling her close and talking gently as she watched the emergency unfold.

'He's barely breathing. He's got a pulse. I'll try oxygenating him first but he might need Narcan.' Charlie grabbed the bag-mask apparatus that was permanently set up, turned on the wall oxygen supply and placed the mask over the man's face.

Carrie felt sick and her heart thundered as she stared at the dusky colour of the stranger's lips visible through the clear plastic of the mask. Large raw sores, bleeding and cracked, blemished the corners.

Rick was frighteningly still. He looked malnourished and unkempt, his hair dirty, his skin pasty. Faint yellowy bruises followed the bluey-green tracks of his knotted, abused veins. He looked like death.

Carrie felt her adrenaline surge as the desperate urgency of a life in the balance played out before her. She recognised Charlie's professional jaw hold as he assisted the struggling respirations of his patient but the direness of the situation was freaking her out. She'd been here before. Seen lips that colour before. She shut out the image and drew in a shaky breath, she had to get out. 'I'll take her outside.'

But the little girl protested more loudly and cried out hysterically for her uncle so Carrie stayed where she was, rooted to the spot, not wanting to watch but unable to look away. The child settled again. 'Poor darling, it's OK. I'm not going to take you away from your Uncle Donny.'

The little one whimpered and hung onto Carrie's neck for dear life. Her hiccoughy breaths were warm against Carrie's neck and she squeezed the little girl closer.

Charlie could hear Carrie's soothing assurances as he assessed Rick's condition. He recognised the tremulous husk in it from last night. Was she spinning out over there, like last night? Would she vomit? Faint? Damn it, he needed to concentrate on this, not her!

Rick wasn't coming round. His lips had pinked up. His saturations were good. He was breathing a little more but still not adequately enough. Charlie grabbed a Narcan minijet from the IV trolley, flipped off the plastic lids and quickly assembled it. Time was of the essence.

He plunged the needle into Rick, administering the narcotic antagonist to reverse the effects of the drug. Rick wasn't going to like it but he was too drugged that oxygen alone would eventually bring him round.

Moments later Rick took a huge gulping breath and then

another. He shook his head from side to side and tried to push Charlie's hands and the mask away. He started to cough, then gag. Charlie and Donny rolled him on to his side and he stilled momentarily. Moments later he started flailing around again and succeeded in ripping the oxygen mask away.

He sat up abruptly and swore a lot.

'Easy,' Charlie said gently.

Rick lurched off the bench. 'God damn it! My hit, man, you wasted my hit.'

Tilly started crying again.

'Shut that kid up,' the man bellowed, and staggered out of the room, knocking over a few chairs on his way out of the clinic.

Donny started after him.

'Let him go,' Charlie said, taking Rick's abuse on the chin. He knew it was hopeless to point out that he'd just saved his life. He'd been saving drug addicts from their overdoses for five years, sometimes as much as one a day, and very few of them were ever grateful. In fact, Rick's behaviour was typical. God knew what he'd had to do to score the money for his hit and *he* had gone and ruined it by injecting a drug that not only sucked up the respiratory depressant effects but also sucked up the euphoric effects.

Carrie stared after the man while she tried to quieten a scared Tilly. 'Doesn't he need to go to hospital?'

'No,' Donny said, leaning heavily against the bed. 'All he needs is to score again.'

Carrie shook her head. Try as she may, she couldn't understand the addict mentality. How could somebody who once upon a time must have been as innocent as the squirming toddler she held in her arms waste it all like that?

Tilly was reaching for her uncle and Carrie held her close a moment longer, gave her an extra-big squeeze then handed her over with still shaking hands.

'You OK?' Charlie asked. She was looking pale again, like she had last night.

She nodded. 'I think I'll just sit down for a bit.'

Charlie watched her walk out of the room and sink into one of the seats in the waiting area. 'You OK?' he asked Donny.

'Sure, but I'd better go. My sister will be starting to wonder what I've done with Tilly.'

'We can't have that, now, can we?' Charlie pulled a face at the little girl and was rewarded with a watery smile. 'Come on, I'll walk you out.'

'Wave goodbye to the nice lady, Tilly,' Donny crooned as they passed where Carrie was sitting.

''Night, Tilly.' Carrie smiled at the toddler, suddenly desperately missing her own little girl as Tilly gave her a shy wave. This was a whole different world—grungy and gritty and real—and she was pleased her child would never be exposed to it.

Carrie watched Charlie and Donny walking to the door, their deep voices hushed but reaching her nonetheless.

'You taking your medication?' Charlie asked.

'Of course, Doc. I promise. What about you?'

'Absolutely. But it'll be fine, Donny, don't worry. Really.'

'I'm so sorry, Doc…'

They walked outside and Carrie couldn't hear them any longer. Intriguing. Medication for what? Did that have something to do with the tablets she'd seen Charlie taking earlier that day? Sorry about what?

Charlie came back inside and wandered over to stand in front of her. 'You were great with Tilly. Thanks.'

'There'd be something wrong if I wasn't. Little girls are somewhat my specialty these days.'

Charlie chuckled. 'Still, you didn't…'

'What? Choke? Like last night?'

He smiled. 'I was going to say freeze, but if you prefer choked…'

Carrie smiled. 'Don't judge me on what happened last night. I'm afraid I'm just not a clinician.'

But she was so good with Tilly. She'd been scared but he'd also heard compassion in her voice, seen it in the way she'd held the toddler close. And the way she had held that wound last night had been the epitome of professional technique. Maybe she was being too harsh on herself? 'Really? Why? Did something happen?'

Carrie stood up. She couldn't talk about this with a stranger. She found it hard enough to discuss with her nearest and dearest. 'It's just not me. I'm not…good with people…with patients. Fortunately I found that out early. Goodnight. See you in the morning.'

Carrie was at the door when his words halted her.

'He died, you know. Three hours after getting to hospital.'

Her hand stilled on the handle. 'Yes, I know,' she said, and walked out the door.

Charlie ran his finger back and forth along the rolled plastic edge of the chair where she'd been sitting. Quite the conundrum was Dr Carrie Douglas. She'd said she wasn't good with people yet she'd taken the time to ring the hospital and find out what had happened to the man from last night.

Only the good ones did that.

CHAPTER THREE

BY FRIDAY lunchtime Carrie was looking forward to escaping for two days. The drop-in centre was a very intense place to be. It was full of drifting kids and angry young men and jaded-looking young women. It attracted the drugged, drunk, violent and abusive of all ages. Too many of the faces told a heartbreaking story about the chilling, gritty reality of life on the streets and below the poverty line.

Carrie had just tried to keep out of the way. Charlie had been right. It was utter chaos most days. A crazy three-ring circus. On steroids. It wasn't her job to get involved. Her job was to complete a report for the hospital board on its riskiest enterprise. To establish the viability of the drop-in centre. And it wasn't looking good.

So for the rest of the week she'd stayed in the staffroom, tapping away on her laptop, sorting through mounds of paperwork, ignoring the various noises she heard from the other side of the door. The very loud music, the bad language, the punch-ups, the hysterical girls, the angry parents and the police.

She had also ignored the regular troop of sweaty boys in and out of her work area as she'd worked through lunchtimes. And the sounds of good-natured competition drifting in through the high windows from the court outside. And the angry, tense exchanges that all too often broke out as recreation became serious.

And worst, the disturbing presence of Charlie as he teased, cajoled, laughed, pleaded, reasoned, flattered and coaxed his way into the hearts and minds of a bunch of tough kids living tough lives. It was clear he was well respected by the regulars. Her ears homed in on his strong authoritative voice each lunch-hour as he encouraged and mediated, pushing the teens to be their best.

It sounded just like the voice he'd used with her at the accident scene. Calm. Confident. Positive. Designed to get the most out of a person, the best out of a situation. It put you at ease, made you feel—made you believe—you could do it. And combined with that crooked smile of his and his shaggy, unruly, rock-star hair that flopped endearingly into his eyes, it got results. Heaven knew, he'd managed to bring her back from the frightening grip of escalating panic.

The back door opened and startled her out of her reverie. The usual ragtag crowd jostled through the staffroom, laughing and joking, crowing over who'd won and who'd shot the most baskets.

Charlie and Joe trooped in after them. Joe grinned at her, gulped down a cold bottle of water from the fridge and burped loudly. 'Needed that.' He winked at her. 'Gotta go, Charles. See you next week, Carrie.'

Carrie smiled. 'See ya, Joe.' She watched Joe leave the room and noticed how he signalled to Charlie with his index finger as if indicating the number one and then shot him a thumbs-up. Did he mean Charlie only had to put up with her for one more week?

Charlie rolled his eyes at his friend. 'See you over the weekend.' He was pleased when Joe left. He was more than aware that Carrie had caught Joe's sign language even if she did look baffled as to its meaning.

Carrie waited for the door to close. 'If you think I'll be done in a week, I think you'll be disappointed. You are an incredibly bad bookkeeper.'

Charlie chuckled. 'I know.' The paperwork had gone on hold also.

He looked sweaty and hot, his fringe plastered to his forehead. His crooked smile was sexy as hell. 'It wasn't meant to be funny,' she said coolly, annoyed that she was developing a growing fascination with his smile.

'I know.' He laughed again.

Carrie threw her glasses on the table in exasperation and got out of her chair to stretch her legs and back. 'You know, Charlie, if you spent as much time with the books as you do on the basketball court, things wouldn't be in such a mess.'

Charlie gripped the edge of his locker, his peripheral vision full of Carrie twisting and flexing through her middle, emphasising the arch of her back and pushing her full breasts temptingly against the electric blue silk of her blouse. Her jacket was hanging off the back of her chair and he wished she'd leave the damn thing on.

He rustled around for his meds. 'Being fit is important. It keeps me on the ball. Helps me work better with these kids.'

Carrie flopped out of her stretch, her gaze following his progress to the sink. 'You take this fitness thing seriously, don't you?' she asked as she watched him swallow his pills.

He could feel her heavy whiskey gaze on him as he downed the medication and he had to concentrate on not choking on the tablets. He emptied the glass and turned to face her. 'I do what I can.'

'You do more than most. You take a lot of vitamin supplements.'

'Oh…yeah,' He turned away and placed his glass in the sink. *Vitamins. Right.*

He was lying. She caught a flicker of something in his usually open grey gaze before he turned away abruptly. So what were they if they weren't vitamins? There were at least three tablets he took every lunch-hour.

Angela bustled into the room. 'I'm sorry, Charlie, but Lilly's sick. The school's called. I'm going to have to leave.'

Oh, great! The immunisation clinic. 'She OK?'

Angela shrugged. 'A fever.'

'Pop her in to me later, I'll check her out.'

Angela looked uncertain. 'The immunisation clinic, Charlie.'

'Don't worry, I'll manage. Just go.' He smiled.

'It'll take you twice as long without me,' Angela protested.

'I'll manage. Carrie will help,' Charlie added, and shot his most confident smile at his dubious receptionist.

Carrie gaped. Did he think she didn't have enough on her plate, without doing his work, too? She opened her mouth to give him a piece of her mind but he was looking at her with a plea in his eyes that she found hard to resist.

She shut her mouth and turned her head to look at Angela. The older woman was looking her up and down like she had the first day, her expression registering extreme doubt.

She glanced back at Charlie who gave her a wink and a nod. 'Ah…sure, I can.'

Angela gave her the once-over again and Carrie felt as if she'd been dressed down by the school principal and found wanting.

'You sure?' Angela asked her boss.

'I'll be fine,' Carrie butted in, before Charlie had a chance to answer.

Angela ignored her and repeated the question. 'Are you sure?'

He nodded. 'We'll be fine.'

'OK…thanks. I'll pop in later.'

They watched Angela leave. Carrie was miffed by Angela's lack of faith. She felt like the wallflower with braces at a high school prom.

'You are still a registered doctor, aren't you?' he asked as the door shut.

'Of course,' she said indignantly.

He shrugged. 'Hey, something obviously happened with you. I thought you may have been deregistered.'

Obviously? Was it that obvious? 'Most certainly not,' she said primly, drawing herself up to her full height.

'I'm sorry.' He shrugged. 'I just assumed…'

'Like I assumed about the vitamins?' she asked sweetly.

Charlie gave her a grudging smile. 'Touché. Clinic starts in fifteen minutes.'

Now, this she could handle. Surely? Giving a few needles was hardly the same as lending a hand at an accident scene. No one's life was in the balance. There wouldn't be blood or the horrifying urgency of every second counting. A quick jab, dry a few tears, console a few stressed mothers and send them on their way. Anyone could do it.

The waiting area was crowded with men, women and children of all ages when she walked out on shaky legs. For once the brooding teenagers had been completely driven out of the clinic.

'There's a lot of people out there,' she said, leaning against the doorframe of the treatment room.

He nodded. She'd put her jacket back on and he was grateful for it. The full power suit reminded him why she was there. Which was what he needed after seeing her languorous stretch in the staffroom. 'Angela makes sure the immunisation clinic has a high local profile.'

'You're right, she is indispensable.' Carrie had been more than impressed over the course of the week. Angela was efficient, ran the place with military precision and could stare down a sullen teenager or stoned user better than the scariest sergeant major. Not one regular dared to give Angela any lip.

Charlie gasped dramatically. 'Me, right? Can I get that in writing?'

Carrie smiled. 'Don't let it go to your head.'

Too late. He'd spent the last five nights with her and her damn pinstriped suits in his head. He cleared his throat. 'You handle the paperwork, I'll give the injections,' Charlie said as he checked the vaccine fridge in the treatment room. 'Angela has all the cards out for those she's expecting. They'll be in alphabetical order. Any drop-ins should have their baby books and we can access their information through the practitioner portal at the national immunisation database website. Angela already has it up on the screen.'

He brushed past her, ignoring the brief press of flesh, and strode to the desk, demonstrating quickly how to access the information she'd need and how to update each patient's records.

'Weigh the babies if that hasn't been done in the last month.' He pointed to the scales.

'Right,' she said stiffly, still processing the sigh of her cells as her body reeled from the fleeting contact of his body against hers. Weigh the babies. *See, easy. I can do this.* It was hardly practising medicine.

Charlie stopped and gave her a searching look. 'Are you sure?'

She scrambled to get her head together. She put her hand on her hip and lifted her chin. 'I have two degrees. I think I can manage some data entry and a set of scales.'

Her stance emphasised the dip of her waist and the curve of her hip and her haughty put-down tone had the completely opposite effect. He was anything but put down. 'Right, then, let's get started before the mob starts to revolt.'

Three hours later they had finally broken the back of the queue. Three agonising hours of watching Charlie cluck, cuddle, soothe and generally work magic with every baby, toddler and child in the room. And their mothers. He'd even managed to engage the odd bored, rather-be-shooting-hoops dad who had been dragged along, as well.

He was a natural with kids. They responded to him with that typical childlike exuberance. He pulled faces and put on funny voices and teased and joked with the older children. He wiped away their tears and gave out 'I've Been Beary Brave Today' teddy-bear-shaped stickers and the kids' eyes lit up like he'd just given them diamonds.

She remembered him saying that his wife hadn't wanted children. She also remembered getting the distinct impression that he wasn't keen on them, either. Which was a shame—he really had a way with little people. He'd certainly won Dana's heart with his Sleeping Beauty comment. She hadn't stopped talking about him since.

Her mind drifted to her daughter. And then, as usual, to Dana's father. Why couldn't Rupert have been more like Charlie? The horrible night she had told him about being pregnant, the night he had broken her heart, was never far from her mind. It had been a particularly awful time, coming hot on the heels of her disintegrating medical career. She had loved him and he had rejected her and his baby during the worst time of her life, and with such vehemence, such disdain, part of her had never recovered.

He had become engaged shortly after that and had moved overseas to practise in London. But his betrayal had stayed close to her heart. As long as she lived, she never wanted to be in a position where someone could destroy her again. Love gave other human beings extraordinary power over you and she was never handing that power over again.

She shut the website down with a vehement click, annoyed that she had let her thoughts drift, and surveyed the now empty waiting room. Her feet ached from constant getting up and down and walking back and forth. Her fashionable three-inch stilettos weren't meant for movement. Sitting at a desk, yes, going back and forth, no.

She got off Angela's chair and flopped down on one of the

squishy lounges, kicking her shoes off temporarily and wriggling her toes. She had to get back to the laptop, she was three hours behind, but for a brief moment she let her head flop back and sighed. It felt heavenly.

Charlie stood framed in the doorway, watching her. The clinic had gone well. OK, Carrie hadn't been as fast at things as Angela, but for a novice she'd excelled, and she'd had amazingly good rapport with the clients. Maybe that was a mother thing, an area she could relate to, but he didn't think so. She had great people skills. It seemed such a shame that she was wasting them in management.

He watched her hand creep up and rub absently at her neck. He was hit by an overwhelming urge to give her a shoulder rub. She looked done in. He remembered her stretching earlier. She was, no doubt, used to ergonomically designed chairs and having to contend with a hard plastic seat was probably playing havoc with her spine alignment. She probably had kinks in her kinks.

But even as he thought it he knew how dangerous touching her would be. He'd thought about little else since he'd met her. To have to go home each night and add in the reality of her touch to his dreams would give him a permanent case of insomnia. She'd probably sue him for harassment anyway. He shoved his hands in his pockets and went back to putting the treatment room back to rights.

Carrie heard the door open and almost groaned. A latecomer? She opened her eyes to find a girl, a young woman actually, standing there, looking miserable. She had multicoloured short spiky hair, several facial piercings and sad, sad eyes ringed by thick black eyeliner. She looked about seventeen.

Carrie sat up. 'Are you OK?'

The girl nodded.

'Do you want to see Ch—Dr Wentworth?'

The girl shook her head.

Carrie recognised the look in her eyes. She'd seen it in her mirror often enough. 'You just want to sit for a bit?' Carrie asked, patting the lounge beside her.

The girl eyed the space, strode across the room and flung herself down next to Carrie. 'Men are such pigs,' she said vehemently.

Carrie looked for a response that would encourage the girl to unburden but she'd never been very good at the psychology side of things. And with thoughts of Rupert never far away, what else could she do other than agree?

'This is true.'

The girl looked at her, startled, and then turned back to stare straight ahead. 'They suck.'

True again. 'They do.'

Charlie's ears pricked up at the conversation and he strained to hear more.

'How could they be so…so…duplicitous?'

It was Carrie's turn to be startled this time. She'd mistakenly judged this girl on her appearance. She obviously had an excellent vocabulary. 'It's a Y chromosome thing. I think they go to duplicitous studies while we're at common sense 101,' Carrie sighed.

Charlie wanted to protest on behalf of his sex as he edged closer to the open door.

'More like gullible 101,' the young woman grumbled.

Carrie laughed. 'Perhaps you're right.'

'So what do we do about it?' the girl complained, turning beseeching eyes on Carrie.

Well, now, wasn't that the million-dollar question? Carrie shrugged. 'Believe in yourself. Believe that you're worth more than that. That there's someone out there who will treat you with the respect you deserve, and don't settle for less.'

The girl sagged against the chair. 'Oh.'

'Sorry, probably not what you wanted to hear. If you've got another suggestion, I'd be happy to hear it.'

'I was thinking of making a voodoo doll.'

Carrie laughed. The idea of sticking pins into an effigy of Rupert was inordinately funny. The girl laughed with her.

Charlie winced and made a note to never cross either of them.

'Nah, I suppose you're right,' the girl conceded after a while. 'How long did it take you to figure it out?'

Carrie laughed but there was a harsh edge to it. 'Too long.'

The girl sighed. 'Think I'll become a lesbian.'

'I don't think you get a choice. I think you either are or you aren't.'

She sighed again. 'We'd be better off without them.'

Very mature. But then she thought of Dana's quick girly giggle. And Charlie's slow lazy smile. 'It wouldn't be as fun, though, would it?'

Carrie chatted to the girl for a while longer then excused herself. She was so behind. She'd hoped to get through December's financial statistics today but helping with the clinic had thrown that out the window. She was just going to have to stay on. Dana was having a sleepover at her sister's house tonight with her cousins so there was no need to rush home.

She walked past Charlie's office. He had the door closed and she assumed, hoped, that he was attending to the immunisation clinic's billing paperwork. The thought of going back to her own stack of papers was exceedingly unappealing. She sat at the table, staring at her laptop, and felt suddenly restless.

She gave herself a shake. She didn't have time for restless. The board would not be impressed if the report was late. It could ruin her otherwise unblemished record. She'd already messed up one career. She wasn't going to blow this one. She donned her glasses—they never failed to put her in the right frame of mind.

Charlie opened the door a few minutes later. Carrie looked at him over the top of her rims. Her jacket was off again and he almost turned around and went back to his office to stare at the walls some more.

'It's past five. Shouldn't you be heading off?' He flicked the kettle on.

She shook her head. 'Helping you put me behind so I'm working on tonight. That's OK, isn't it?'

'Sure. I never usually leave till nine-thirty or ten. What about Dana?'

Carrie refused to allow the little thrill of pleasure coursing through her any rein. So, he was thoughtful—that wasn't entirely alien to the male species. 'Sleeping over at her cousin's house tonight.'

'Coffee?'

She shook her head. Heavens, no, she already felt too keyed up.

'You work long hours,' Carrie said. 'I don't see you claiming them on any of your timesheets.'

'I'd love for the centre to be open twenty-four seven but with just me, that's not possible. So I do what I can to open extended hours.' He shrugged. 'It's not like I have anything better to do.'

She watched him pour his drink and stir in two sugars. He sounded like he lived for his work, too. And then she realised she was staring and returned her attention to the screen.

'Sorry I put you behind,' he said, leaning against the sink and taking a sip of his scalding hot double-strength brew.

Carrie stopped tapping on the keys again and smiled, thinking back at her afternoon. 'It's OK. I enjoyed it, actually.'

Charlie nodded. He could tell. 'Maybe that's because you're good at it. People respond to you.'

'Nonsense,' she said, going back to her work. She couldn't afford to let his praise go to her head. She was in management now. That's where her future lay. 'I hardly had any contact at all. Spent most of my time on that damn computer.'

He pushed away from the sink and strolled towards her. 'Rubbish. They're a tough crowd, Carrie. Trust me, they liked you. Just look at Tina earlier. She's one seriously mixed-up, closed-off kid. You had her eating out of your hand.'

'Tina? Was that her name? She's a smart girl, that one, she'll figure it out.'

He nodded. 'Thanks in part to you.'

Their eyes met. He could see the wariness in her gaze. The denial. And then the phone rang.

Carrie broke eye contact and stared dumbly at the object hanging on the wall. The damn thing rang all day, constantly interrupting her concentration. She was learning to tune it out.

'That'll be for you,' she said, and watched as he ambled over with his long-legged stride.

'Hello, Valley Drop-In Centre, this is Charlie.'

'Is there something wrong with using your full medical title? Really, Charles, the Wentworth name is something most doctors in Brisbane would kill to have.'

Charlie gripped the receiver tighter. 'Father.'

Carrie looked up from the keyboard. Charlie's dad? He looked and sounded about as pleased to hear from him as he had the day she'd walked in. She didn't know anyone who used such a formal title in everyday conversation.

'Have you looked at that application I emailed you? With my recommendation you'd get the position easily.'

'I'm not having this conversation again. I have a job. I'm not interested in a surgical position.'

Charlie's voice was terse and Carrie looked back at the screen, pretending she couldn't hear every word he was saying.

'Charles! Every Wentworth since—'

'Since federation has risen to the level of consultant in his or her chosen specialty,' Charlie ended, used to the spiel by now.

'You think this is amusing, Charles?'

Good lord, no. His father was about as funny as a wet

week. But, on the other hand, it was getting kind of ridiculous. 'Mildly.'

'I'm thinking of what's best for you Charles.'

'Nonsense. You're thinking of the family reputation. Hell, Dad, the Wentworths aren't the Mafia.' *Although it was beginning to feel like it.* 'Give it up.'

The Wentworths? *The* Wentworth family? Charlie was one of Brisbane's first family? Medical royalty? What the hell was he doing here, in a lowly drop-in clinic?

'We'll speak more about this at lunch on Sunday.'

'Oh, goody,' he said derisively.

'Your mother is expecting you, Charles. Goodbye.'

Charlie hung up on his father's reproachful tone. He glanced at Carrie tapping away at her keyboard, looking for all the world like she wasn't actually there. He chuckled. 'It's OK, Carrie, it was kind of hard not to hear.'

Carrie gave up the pretence. 'You're one of *the* Wentworths?'

'Afraid so.'

Good. It was good that she'd found this out now. Charlie Wentworth was way out of her league. Had she been interested. Which she wasn't. 'So that makes you…'

Charlie nodded. 'The black sheep.'

She gave him a quelling look. 'Ignatius Wentworth's son? Sir Nelson Wentworth's grandson?'

'Guilty.'

The smile he shot her was slow and lazy and her toes curled. *Stop it!* Charlie's family had an entire national research facility named after them, for crying out loud. And she was most definitely a girl from the wrong side of the tracks. 'How the hell did you wind up here? Did you kill someone?'

Charlie was momentarily shocked at her bluntness. And he laughed as she clapped her hand over her mouth to stifle her quick horrified gasp at her unprofessional comment.

'I'm sorry…that didn't quite come out the way I'd planned. Forgive me.'

Charlie sobered. 'It's OK, and, no, I didn't kill someone. I'm here through choice.'

'Choice? Wentworths don't choose grungy drop-in centres.'

'That would be why I'm the black sheep.' He grinned.

Carrie shook her head. 'I don't understand. You could be doing anything.'

Charlie looked at the utter disbelief in her face. Veronica had looked at him like that. Often. Had said the same words. Somehow he'd thought Carrie was different and the thought that she wasn't was strangely depressing. He pulled up a chair and sank into it, taking a swig of his coffee.

'There was an incident when I was a med student. I was on a ride-along shift with the ambulance and we got called to the valley to an overdose. When we arrived there was this girl, she was about my age. And it was cold, you know the middle of winter, so cold. We were all rugged up and she was wearing this tiny T-shirt and miniskirt.' He shook his head, still staring at his coffee.

'No one knew her. I mean, there was this crowd of people around her, gawking at her like she was an exhibit in a museum, but no one knew her. She had tracks all up her arms. A junkie. We tried to revive her but it was too late. We declared her deceased and everyone just drifted away. No one cared. She was just a faceless street kid all alone at the very end with no one to grieve for her. No one to mourn the waste.'

Carrie shivered as she listened to Charlie recount the story. He was staring into the murky depths of his coffee, a far-away look in his cloudy grey gaze.

'And it's stuck with me ever since. I don't know.' He shrugged, looking up at her. 'Maybe it was her age, maybe it was her dead-looking eyes, but all I could think was, there but for the grace of

God…you know? And I just knew, right there at that moment, I knew I had to do something to help kids like that.'

There was silence for a few moments as they stared at each other. It was a moment when Carrie felt she could almost see into his soul. Everything was laid bare to her. There was compassion and righteousness and belief. How would she feel if Dana went off the rails and ran away from home, got into drugs? She could only hope there would be a Charlie with a blanket somewhere, looking out for her.

A few more moments ticked by. 'So, your father's not thrilled?'

Charlie chuckled and downed the remnants of his drink, 'You could say that,' he said, rising and heading for the sink.

Carrie's mobile phone rang. 'It's my mother.'

Charlie nodded and headed out of the room to give her some privacy. 'See you later.'

At nine o'clock Carrie was satisfied enough with her progress to call it a day. She packed up her laptop, grabbed her bag and threw her jacket over her arm.

'I'm off,' she said, leaning against Charlie's doorjamb.

Charlie looked up. She'd applied some more lip gloss and her electric blue silk tempted him with its delectable contents. 'I'll walk you out,' he said, feigning interest in a journal article as he rose.

She shook her head. 'Don't be silly. I'll be fine.'

He gave her a stern look. 'This is the valley. The dodgy end. Daytime, fine. Nighttime, no way.'

Carrie laughed to hide her consternation. Her heartbeat kicked up a notch. Charlie's aura was too disturbing. She gestured with her arm. 'Lead the way.'

They walked side by side the short distance to the back alley where they both parked their cars. His beat-up old Datsun obscured her car temporarily, which was just as well.

'Oh, no,' she gasped, dropping her briefcase in horror.

Her hire car had been stripped and vandalised.

'God damn it!' Charlie shook his head, inspecting the damage. Her wheels were missing, the windows had been smashed and the seats slashed. 'This is why I don't bring the Beamer.'

'You have a BMW?' Carrie asked, temporarily forgetting about her car.

'A present from my parents,' he dismissed.

Of course. 'How tragic for you.'

Charlie ignored her. 'Were there any valuables in it?'

She shook her head. 'Because it was a rental there was nothing in there of ours. Oh, except…' Carrie quickly checked the empty back seat '…Dana's car seat.'

Charlie looked at her. 'I'll buy you another one.'

Carrie groaned and turned to lean against the remnants of her car, trying not to think about the insurance excess she'd be facing. She earned good money but her mortgage was hefty and she always ran fairly close to the wire.

'Come on,' Charlie said, putting his arm around her shoulder and urging her away from the car. 'We'll call the police, file a report and I'll drive you home.'

Carrie resisted the urge to put her head against his shoulder. Just. 'I can catch a taxi.'

'No, wouldn't hear of it,' he insisted. 'It's the least I can do, considering your car was more than likely vandalised by some of my clients.'

Carrie was relieved that Charlie had taken over. She sat in the lounge chair and accepted the cup of tea he'd made for her. The police came promptly due, no doubt, to Charlie's close working relationship with them, and she gave them her details.

'Did you say Swenson Street, miss?'

Carrie nodded at the policeman, who looked like he'd just

graduated from high school. She had to concentrate hard on his questions because Charlie was sitting casually on the fat, squishy arm of her chair and his leg swung lazily in her peripheral vision.

'We've just been there. Your burglar's struck again.'

'"Your" burglar?' Charlie asked, sitting up straighter.

Burglar? Good grief, it made it sound like there was a master jewel thief at large. 'We have a gnome-napper terrorising the street. Old Mrs Dennis's gnomes are mysteriously disappearing.'

'Ah.' Charlie nodded. 'Poor Mrs Dennis.'

Carrie could see the twinkle of mirth lighting his grey eyes, like the sun shining through rainclouds. 'Yes, Swenson Street, just like living in the Bronx,' she agreed gravely.

The police left and Carrie and Charlie argued over his offer of a lift. The clinic was dark, Charlie having turned off all the lights in preparation to leave. The streetlights bathed the lounge in a soft glow.

'Don't you trust me?'

He was standing behind her and his voice was soft, a seductive caress reaching through the gloom to touch her across the short distance that separated them. That was the crazy thing. She did trust him. She felt perfectly safe. But there was a frisson of something else, too. A slight tremble to her hand and huskiness in her breath when she thought about sharing a car with him. Something stirred inside that hadn't been stirred in a long time. Something that had been breathed into life five nights ago.

'Don't be ridiculous.' She gave a half-laugh. 'Of course I do and because it's Friday night in the city, and I can't be bothered to wait an hour for a taxi, you've got yourself a deal.'

Carrie's mobile rang as she did her seat belt up and she answered it. Charlie buckled up, too, started the car and pulled out as Carrie was hanging up.

Charlie's male scent filled the confines of the car and Carrie had to resist the urge to put her face against his neck and inhale deeper. What the hell was happening to her? She was sitting in a car with a man she barely knew, getting high on pheromones. She just didn't do stuff like this.

'That was my sister,' she said into the silence, grabbing hold of anything, anything to stop her actually sniffing his neck. 'She was just ringing to remind me about my hair appointment tomorrow,' she prattled. 'She's a hairdresser,' she prattled some more.

Charlie pulled out of the alley. 'Yeah? Maybe I'll drop by one day and get that sensible haircut my father keeps nagging me about.'

'Oh, no,' Carrie admonished immediately, and raised a hand to touch his hair. It was soft and fine and the glide of it through her fingers was a surprisingly sensual experience.

Then she realised what she was doing and dropped her hand abruptly. 'It suits you,' she said, covering for the heat that she felt flushing her cheeks.

Charlie's scalp tingled where she'd touched it and his thoughts were temporarily scrambled.

'Warm in here, isn't it?' she muttered, winding the window down.

'Yes,' Charlie agreed, winding his window down also. There was a vibe between them that was hard to ignore. He could see the quickened rise and fall of her chest, the pull of the fabric across her breasts, her lips glistening in the passing glow of the streetlights.

And in his mind's eye he could see her pulling the clasp out of her hair, discarding her glasses and him hauling her into his seat, onto his lap, ripping open that sexy, silky shirt, the buttons popping everywhere. He gripped the steering-wheel harder.

Thankfully the trip to her place was brief and she was content to stare out the window and not converse. He was excruciatingly conscious of her anyway, he didn't need her voice in his ear. He should have let her take a taxi. He switched the engine off. *Just walk her to the door, Charlie, see her inside and turn around.*

Carrie unclipped her seat belt and heard a chorus of alarm bells ringing in her head as Charlie also unclipped his and opened his door. She placed a stilling hand on his arm. 'You don't have to see me in.'

Her hand felt hot through the fabric of his shirt and he wondered how hot it would feel on other areas of his body. 'What about the burglar?'

She gave a half-laugh, hoping desperately to lighten the atmosphere. 'The gnome-napper? You're kidding, right?'

He looked at her building, at the lush tropical jungle that seemed to occupy every piece of land. Anyone could conceal themselves in the dense foliage. 'I'll see you in anyway.' He climbed out of the car and away from her hot little hand.

Carrie took a deep breath and exited the car also. She was ultra-conscious of him behind her for the short trip from the street through the gardens to her front door.

'Right, well, as you can see, no one lurking in the bushes. You can go now,' she said briskly digging around in her bag for her keys.

Charlie looked at her. She sounded like a schoolteacher dismissing a child. He remembered how intimate it had felt the last time he'd been standing at her front door, holding Dana.

'Aren't you going to invite me in for a nightcap?'

She stopped her search and looked at him. *Was he mad?* 'No.'

He chuckled. 'A coffee?'

Stark raving obviously. 'Coffee keeps me awake,' she said primly.

And she was seriously going to be able to sleep with this hum happening between them? He was going to lie awake, thinking of her straddled across him in his car, her blouse torn open. 'Breakfast?' He grinned.

Carrie felt her stomach lurch and heat flush her face, and was thankful for the night's dark shadows. She opened her mouth to issue a stinging retort and noticed the teasing look on his face. 'Are you trying to sexually harass me, Charlie?'

He laughed. 'Is it working?'

Apparently. If the low-level buzz that was sensitising long-forgotten parts of her body was any indication. This was so not a conversation they should be having. She triumphantly pulled her keys out of her bag. 'Thanks for the lift. My bed's calling.'

Yes, it was. He could hear it loud and clear. He watched her shut her eyes briefly as she realised that she'd said something she shouldn't have. Her bed was out there now. 'Right.' He swallowed. 'I should go.'

Carrie looked into his eyes and nodded, trying to forget her gaffe. Hell. Why had she mentioned her bed? 'Yes,' she said.

Neither of them moved.

Put the key in the door and go inside. 'Thanks again…for the…lift,' she said. His intense stare made her trip and stumble over the words.

Turn around now and go back to the car. 'My pleasure,' he said, staring at her mouth beckoning him, bewitching him. How much pleasure could he find in those glistening, delectable lips?

Carrie didn't move a muscle. She couldn't—even her diaphragm was having trouble performing its usual function. She was conscious only of his eyes and the way he was looking at her mouth. Her breath was uneven and her heart fluttered madly.

He took a step closer to her. She felt suffocated by his nearness, by the intensity of his gaze, by the flare of hunger she could see in his grey eyes. Had anyone ever looked at her with such naked need? She took a step back. The door stopped her retreat.

An inner voice warned Charlie against the next step he took. But he was too far gone, too caught up in the pout of her mouth and the smell of her and the catch of her breath. 'Tell me to leave,' his husky voice requested.

'Leave,' she whispered, her whole body tingling in anticipation, her gaze fixed on his mouth. His eyes were hooded now as his tall, broad frame blocked out the ambient light.

He shook his head. 'Mean it,' he whispered back.

CHAPTER FOUR

THERE was a brief moment when meaning it was possible but it passed and Carrie knew she wasn't strong enough to turn him away. The thought of his lips on hers, his hand on her body, his stubble grating erotically against her cheek was making a mockery of her self-control.

His head was moving closer to hers. All she needed to do was lean forward a little and their bodies would be in intimate contact. But only the slow passage of his mouth registered to her severely dysfunctional brain.

Her eyes fluttered closed at the first touch of his lips on hers and then everything imploded. It was no gentle, explorative press of flesh. It was hot and hard and frantic. Bordering on desperate. Carrie felt the heat instantly. Everywhere. All the way through to her centre and back out again.

He was everywhere. His breadth surrounded her, over-whelmed her, demanding and achieving entry into her most prized possession—her personal space. He pushed her harder and harder against the door, her back flattening against the wood as she pushed against him, inviting a deepening of the passion raging between them.

She couldn't be passive—his lips demanded her to be an active participant. To thrust her tongue against his, to moan, to clutch the front of his shirt, to breathe hard like she'd run a marathon, to grind her hips into his. There was no time for thought or reflection, there was just feeling.

Like how good his mouth felt against hers, how her breasts ached to be touched, how hard he felt as he rocked his pelvis into her. And how long it had been since she'd done this. How ready she was. And how this kiss was never, ever going to be enough.

She wanted more. She wanted to see all of him. Touch all of him. Feel him deep inside her. There were no thoughts of tomorrow or Dana or her job. It had been four long years and his kisses were like sweet wine on parched lips. She couldn't think straight. Just feel. Just experience. Just drink up every drop.

She dragged her mouth away. 'Inside,' she croaked.

'Yes,' he said, his breath coming in harsh gulps. He whisked the keys out of her fingers and made short work of the barrier to her bed. Hell, he'd have kicked it in if it had been required.

He swept her off her feet and cut off her startled yelp with his mouth as he nudged the door shut with his foot. She kissed like a fallen angel, sweet and sinful, and he wondered if she made love like one, too. *He had to have her—now.*

'Which way?' he demanded in a rough voice. She pointed and he strode quickly towards the indicated room, kissing her roughly before throwing her on the bed.

Light from a streetlamp outside entered through the high window above the bed. She looked utterly gorgeous, lying there, thoroughly kissed, on the mattress. Her mouth was swollen and moist, tendrils of her auburn hair had escaped the clasp and her skirt had ridden up her thighs. He needed to see her naked. Quickly.

He lowered himself down, planting a knee between her legs, and felt himself harden further as her hips ground against it. He pushed his knee hard against her and smiled at the moan that escaped her lips. He grasped her shoulders and pulled her over with him.

And then his head hit a hard plastic object and it roared to life, throwing a kaleidoscope of colours around the room. 'Twinkle, Twinkle, Little Star' blared out in a piercing electronic voice. The fact that her body was lying on top of his, pressing and rubbing in all the right places, was temporarily forgotten.

It was like a bucket of cold water. The bucket of cold water he needed. *What the hell are you doing?* He moved abruptly out from underneath her, displacing her.

'Sorry,' Carrie said, groping for Dana's favourite toy, her body already lamenting the distance. Her mouth and her breasts tingled. The buzz intensified, demanding to be sated.

'No…I'm sorry…' Charlie ran a frustrated hand through his hair. What the hell was he doing? What the hell had happened to his iron-clad self-control? He couldn't do this. He still had over a week before he got his test results. *And she had a kid.* And even if he had been stupid enough to make one exception in this whole crazy year, he didn't even have condoms with him. He deliberately didn't carry them any more, so temptation was always kept at bay. He had to get out of there. Now.

Carrie found the 'off' button and the silence was suddenly deafening.

'Dana's?' he asked, automatically looking at the offending toy while his mind frantically groped for a way out.

'Yes,' she said, standing and placing it in the basket beside her bed. She could tell by the way his gaze kept sliding to the doorway that there would be no more kissing tonight. She cringed, thinking about how easy she'd been. How desperate she must have seemed. And still every cell in her body hummed with arousal and she railed against her body's betrayal.

God, what a mess. She looked so lovely, so desirable in the subdued light he wanted to push her back on the mattress and finish what he'd started. He clenched his fists to stop himself following through. 'I'm sorry…' he said, his breathing still ragged. 'I have to go. I'm sorry…things got out of hand. I can't do this.'

'It's OK, I understand,' she dismissed, injecting a briskness into her voice that required supreme effort. Damn him to hell. Why did he have to tease her with the possibilities, and then snatch them away before she'd experienced their full potential?

Charlie drew a shaky hand through his hair. His body was still aroused and he was teetering on the edge, while she'd gone back to being Ms Pinstripe again. Ms Untouchable. For a moment there he'd had Ms Tie-Dye back, Ms Touch-Me-Everywhere, and he knew which one he preferred. How could she morph so quickly?

'I don't think you do.'

Carrie shrugged. 'It was a reality check. A lot of men don't want to get involved with single mothers.'

Was that what she thought? He opened his mouth to deny it and then shut it again. This thing between them was crazy. His life was on hold. And even if it came off hold next week, he didn't need anything heavy in his life for a very long time. Perhaps never. And what did he have to offer a single mother and her daughter? He sure as hell didn't have any great parenting examples to draw on. Maybe it was best for her to think the worst of him?

He reached out to touch her shoulder, dropping his hand when she took a step back. 'I'm sorry,' he said.

She heard the genuine note of regret in his voice and couldn't bear it. She was frustrated and humiliated and just wanted to be alone. 'Just go.'

Carrie heard the door close a few moments later. She kicked her shoes off and threw herself down on the bed, pulling her legs up into a foetal position, trying to ease the ache between them. Damn him, damn Charles Wentworth to hell.

How stupid was she? Had she learnt nothing from the whole Rupert disaster? How could she fall for the attentions of another posh doc? What the hell would he ever see in a girl from the wrong side of the tracks? No breeding. No pedigree. She'd had a child out of wedlock, for heaven's sake. It'd be Rupert all over again. OK to warm his bed at every available opportunity, but not to promise until death did them part. Not to take home to meet Mummy and Daddy.

Thank goodness for Dana's toy. If they hadn't been interrupted she had no doubt that she would have gone all the way with Charlie. What the hell had she been thinking? She had to work with him. Probably put him out of business if the books were anything to go by. It was unprofessional. Probably unethical. Certainly it presented a complete conflict of interest.

How was she ever going to face him again?

But face him she did. In her usual no-nonsense, tackle-things-head-on, hard-headed businesswoman manner.

'Morning, Charlie,' she said briskly on Monday morning, striding into his office and standing her briefcase on his desk. 'Don't say anything. Just listen. Friday night was a mistake. We both know it. Let's just mark it down to stupidity and forget it ever happened. OK?'

Charlie blinked. *Stupidity?* 'OK…'

'Good.'

Carrie picked up her briefcase, pivoted on her heel and strode out of his office. It wasn't until she sank down into her chair in the staffroom that she gave her shaking legs and thundering heartbeat any attention. She took a deep breath and congratulated herself on her performance. She flipped open her laptop lid, resolutely putting Friday night behind her and ignoring the betraying tremble of her fingers as they tapped at the keyboard.

Charlie stared after Carrie for a long time. He was still staring when Joe waltzed in with two mugs of coffee.

'One week to go,' Joe said cheerily.

Charlie refocused on his friend's face. 'What?'

'One more week,' Joe repeated, pulling up a chair, propping his feet on the desk and leaning back. 'You know. The blood test. No more pills. The end of twelve months of celibacy.'

'Oh, that.'

Joe sat up straighter. 'Yes, that. You know the HIV thing? The thing that's thrown you for a loop, put your life on hold for an entire year?'

'Mmm.' Charlie said, preoccupied by thoughts of Carrie's moan when he'd pressed his knee hard against her. Thoughts he was supposed to be putting behind him.

Joe cocked an eyebrow. Something screwy was going on. His friend seemed very distracted this morning. 'OK, what's up?' He blew on his drink and took a swig.

Charlie realised he'd only been half listening to Joe. He sighed. 'I ended up in Carrie's bed on Friday night.'

Joe almost spat the contents of his mouth all over Charlie's desk. He coughed and spluttered as he struggled to swallow. 'Hell. I hope you've started carrying condoms again.'

Charlie shook his head. 'Nope.'

'Did you…?'

'No. We were interrupted…thank God.'

Joe whistled. 'So I guess it's going to be weird around here now?'

Charlie shook his head. 'Apparently not. She's just marched in here all prim and proper and announced that it was a mistake. That we should put it behind us and move on.'

Joe chuckled. 'Well, that's very mature of her.'

Charlie saw the amused twinkle in his friend's eyes and shook his head. 'Pain in the butt. Both of you.'

Joe gave a full-on laugh this time. 'So it was good, huh?'

Charlie threw Joe a quelling look. 'That's not the point.'

'Come on, man. Twelve months. Three hundred and sixty-five days. Without it. Without any action whatsoever. It must have been sweet.'

Charlie felt his loins stir with hot memories. *Sweet as sugar.* 'That's not the point,' he reiterated.

Joe sobered and placed his coffee on the table. 'Look, you have to break the drought with someone when you get your tests come back negative. Why not Carrie? She's a great girl. She even wears pinstripes.'

Charlie looked at his friend with exasperation. 'What did I tell you when Veronica and I split up?'

'You were never doing the whole commitment thing again as long as you lived?'

'Right.'

'So?'

'So, Carrie has commitment written all over her. She has a four-year-old child. I don't know the first thing about being a father, a good one anyway, let alone to a child that's not my own.'

'Rubbish. You're great with kids. Just take whatever your father did and do the opposite,' Joe stated.

Charlie shot him a quelling look. 'You're not listening. She's not a drought-breaker girl. She's a hot roast dinners and slippers by the fire girl.'

Joe winked at him. 'Who just happens to look hot in pinstripes.'

'Joe! Work with me here.'

He laughed. 'Charlie, relax. I think you're getting a little ahead of yourself, don't you?'

Charlie shook his head. 'No. That's the point. She has commitments, big commitments. She can't just be a quick roll in the hay. I can't think about sleeping with her without looking at the bigger picture.'

Joe shook his head. 'How the hell you grew up to be so honourable in your family I have no idea.'

Charlie ignored him. 'I think she's been pretty messed up

by her ex. And she's auditing me, for goodness' sake. She could put me out of business.'

Joe laughed. 'Ah, living on the edge. A turn-on, isn't it?'

Charlie sighed and shut his eyes, letting his head flop back. 'You're incorrigible.'

'OK, OK, no Carrie. But promise when the tests come back negative we'll have a night on the town. Like the old days. You just need to get back on the horse, man. Find an outlet for all those pent-up tadpoles.'

Charlie opened his eyes. His friend was right. It was just the abstinence making him crazy. It wasn't the memory of how good Carrie had felt, her softness pressed against him or her fiery response to his kisses. It had been a year of denying himself those base, natural male urges and throwing all of himself into his work to forget about Veronica and the divorce and offsetting the nagging worry that he might have contracted a terminal illness. A terminal illness with a really bad stigma.

'You've got a deal.' Charlie held out his hand and they shook on it.

Carrie was doing really well until lunchtime when the usual troop of teenagers interrupted her concentration. She'd ruthlessly clamped down on the memories that had played in her head all weekend like a projector reel stuck in a rut. She'd been powering through Charlie's business activity statements, determined to cut her time at the clinic as short as possible. Her face burned every time her mind drifted to Friday night. How could she have allowed him such liberties?

She looked up and caught his furtive glance as he walked through the staffroom. Their eyes locked and suddenly she was back to Friday night, pinned against her door, his heat all around her, his tongue demanding entry to her mouth. Her breasts were tingling, her breath becoming thick and husky.

'Carrie.' He nodded.

'Charlie.' She nodded back.

Get a grip! She expelled a breath as he joined the others. *Why?* Why, oh, why was her body betraying her over this? Charlie Wentworth was out of her league. He'd practically run screaming from the room when the reality of Dana had intruded into their sexual bubble. He could never be a part of her life. *Their lives. Their lives. Hers and Dana's.* Single mothers couldn't afford the luxury of thinking only about themselves.

And since when had men even factored into her life? Since Rupert anyway? The last four years had been about Dana and building a career to support her daughter, to make her daughter proud. She hadn't taken her eye off that ball once. Until Friday night. And now there was this whole other world out there. And it was lonely.

The phone rang and Carrie resolutely ignored it. Her concentration had been shot all afternoon and she had half an hour to go. It stopped ringing and she thanked Charlie silently. Angela had left a couple of hours ago and the responsibility of answering the phones fell to Charlie.

The door opened and Carrie braced herself for the impact of Charlie's presence. He picked up the wall phone, held it out to her.

'Your nanny's on the line.'

Carrie rose quickly from her seat. Something must be wrong. Susie was not a panicker. Why hadn't she rung her mobile? She flipped open her mobile to discover the battery was dead. Damn it. Had she been that distracted over the weekend that she'd forgotten to recharge it last night?

She took the receiver from him. Instantly she could hear Dana screaming in the background. 'Susie?'

'Carrie, I'm sorry to ring you at work, I tried your mobile

but it kept saying it was switched off. Dana's fallen and cracked her chin on the pot plant and I think it's going to need stitching.'

For a crazy second Carrie's heart stopped. Nothing, nothing had ever happened to Dana other than the odd bruise. She could hear her daughter's distress and her maternal instinct roared into overdrive. 'Is she OK? Did she hit her head? Was she knocked unconscious?'

Charlie heard the note of concern heighten Carrie's voice and quirked an eyebrow at her.

'No,' Susie said reassuringly. 'She's fine. She's just worked herself up because of the blood. And I'm afraid this is one situation where nanny kisses aren't going to cut it.'

Blood? 'Is it bleeding a lot?' Carrie asked, trying not to let Dana's crying or the image of her blood oozing out everywhere affect her.

Charlie walked towards her, concern in his grey gaze. She wanted to huddle into his chest and draw strength from his tall, lean frame. She wished she was at home. What the hell was she doing here with books that were a mess and a man who had rejected her?

She wanted to put her hand down the phone and drag her daughter to her breast. Assure herself immediately that Dana was really as OK as Susie seemed to think.

'Not any more, but it did. The wound isn't very big but it's really gaping.'

Carrie's brain quickly sorted through the possibilities as she watched Charlie draw nearer. By the time she got home and they went to either the GP or the hospital it would be another hour. Susie would have to take her and she could meet them there. But it was getting close to rush-hour.

'What's wrong?' Charlie asked quietly.

Carrie put her hand over the mouthpiece, her hand trembling slightly. 'Dana needs stitches in her chin.'

'Bring her here. I'll do it.'

Carrie looked at him blankly for a few moments.

'At this hour of the day your nanny will probably be able to make it here quicker. Unless you'd rather someone else did it?'

Carrie continued to look at him blankly.

'Trust me, I do a lot of stitching. I stitch like a pro. My father's right, I should definitely be a surgeon.'

He gave her one of his slow sexy smiles and she saw that confidence in his eyes. The one from the accident scene and the overdosed drug addict. And she knew she could trust him with this. 'Bring her here, Susie. Dr Wentworth has offered to do the suturing.'

'How brave is she?' Charlie asked when Carrie had hung up the phone.

'She's pretty good. She's not one of those hysterical little girls. If we explain how important it is that she stays still, I reckon she'll be OK.'

'All right, then.' He smiled. 'I'll go and get set up.'

Carrie paced the front lounge area, the thump of music from the jukebox grating on stretched nerves. Where were they? It had been nearly half an hour.

'Mummy!'

Carrie felt her heart contract as she saw Susie, clutching a bloodied and bandaged Dana in her arms. Her daughter's T-shirt was spotted with dried blood and there was a smear of blood on her forehead. She met them on the pavement and squeezed her daughter close.

'I hurted my chin, Mummy.'

Carrie laughed. 'Well, you obviously didn't knock your noggin.' She pulled out of the embrace to inspect her daughter's injury. It was covered with a sticking plaster so the damage was hard to assess. 'Come on, let's get you inside to Charlie.'

'Charlie?' Dana's eyes lit up like light bulbs. 'From the crash?'

'Yes.' Carrie laughed. 'Charlie from the crash.'

Carrie cherished the happy hug Dana bestowed on her as she made for the treatment room.

'Ah, here she is, my little Sleeping Beauty.'

Dana giggled at Charlie and Carrie felt warm all over at how naturally her daughter responded to him. She only hoped Dana felt the same way after Charlie had injected local anaesthetic into her wound site!

'Hello, Charlie,' Dana chirped.

'Hello, Sleeping Beauty. What have you been doing to yourself?'

'I felled over. Susie says I never look where I'm going.'

Carrie's laugh was joined by Charlie's warm chuckle. 'Grown-ups are such spoilsports. Not looking where you're going is so much more fun.'

Dana giggled again and Carrie was pleased Susie had already departed. Her daughter looked so small sitting on the big bench, her legs dangling over the edge, her white sandals with red butterflies swinging back and forth. Her blonde hair was pulled up into two bunches sitting high on her head, a yellow ribbon around each one.

She looked at Charlie, at the world, with such trust in those big blue eyes and Carrie felt irrational mother's guilt rear its ugly head. If she'd had been there maybe this wouldn't have happened.

'OK, now, I need to have a look at your chin. Do you want Mummy or me to pull the plaster off?'

Dana looked solemnly from one to the other. 'Mummy,' she announced.

Carrie smiled and kissed Dana on the head. 'Fast or slow, baby?'

'Fast,' Dana replied.

Carrie peeled up a corner of the plaster. 'OK, ready… steady…'

'Go!' Dana pronounced.

Carrie ripped it off quickly without a peep from Dana. 'Ugh,' she said, looking at the gaping hole beneath. 'That definitely needs fixing.'

Dana nodded. 'Naughty pot plant.'

Charlie chuckled and sat on a mobile stool in front of Carrie's daughter and snapped some gloves on. 'Can I have a look, Sleeping Beauty?'

Dana giggled. 'You can fix it, can't you, Charlie?'

Charlie felt his heart melt at Dana's four-year-old innocence. Her big blue eyes were irresistibly gorgeous. So this was how it would be to have your own child, your own flesh and blood, looking at you like you were Superman. Could he fix it? At the moment he could have slain a dragon for her.

He tilted her chin up and examined the damage. The cut wasn't very deep and only about a centimetre long, but gaped in the middle. It had stopped bleeding. 'I reckon I can fix that as good as new.' The wound edges were straight, which would make for a neat scar.

'Susie says that you sew it up just like Grandma does when she sews my buttons back on.'

'Susie is very smart,' Charlie confirmed. 'Open your mouth, sweetie.' Charlie smiled as Dana obeyed instantly, opening it as wide as it could go. Her neat white teeth all appeared to be intact. 'Now, bite down, like this.' Charlie demonstrated. 'Like you're eating a great big steak.'

Dana followed suit. Her bite seemed even enough. He felt along her jaw up to the angle both sides. 'Well, I don't think you did any more damage.'

He glanced at up at Carrie to confirm it. She was looking at him with such an intense stare that he momentarily forgot about Dana sitting in front of him. He momentarily forgot to breathe.

'Charlie.'

Charlie could hear Dana's high voice but Carrie's stare was distracting in the extreme.

'Charlie!' Dana tugged at his sleeve.

'Sorry, sweetie,' he said, breaking eye contact with Carrie. 'Let's get you sewn up.' He stood up and walked over to the tray of instruments he'd prepared earlier, taking deep cleansing breaths. What the hell had that look been about? He didn't know what it meant but he did know that he hadn't been able to look away.

When he'd turned around again, Carrie had helped Dana lie back, her head right at the end of the table, and was fussing around, getting her in position.

'OK, Dana,' he said, rolling a trolley towards the bed and dragging the stool around to the head, 'what's your favourite thing in the whole world?' He snapped the light on above her head. It was attached to the wall via a long angled arm.

Dana giggled. 'That's easy. It's my mummy.'

Good choice, kid. 'What else?'

Dana looked at her mother for an answer. Carrie smiled and shrugged. 'Hmm…I think…oh, ding rolls.'

Charlie raised an eyebrow at Carrie.

'Spring rolls. She loves Chinese takeaway.'

'Ah.' He nodded. 'My favourite, too. What do you want to be when you grow up?'

'A ballerina.'

'Ah.' Charlie winked at Carrie. 'So you like to dance?'

Dana nodded vigorously and sighed. 'I love it.'

Charlie double-gloved and Carrie raised a quizzical eyebrow. 'Second nature around here,' he said dismissively.

Carrie nodded. She supposed it would be in a place where drug addicts with who knew what needed regular resuscitation.

'Now.' He returned his attention to Dana. 'I'll do you a deal,' he said, flicking the bubbles out of the syringe full of local anaesthetic. 'If you can lie nice and still for me while I fix your chin, I'll let you dance to my jukebox.'

'What's a dukebox?' Dana asked.

'Jukebox. Like in *Happy Days*,' Carrie explained.

Dana's eyes lit up. 'You have your very own dukebox, Charlie? Really?'

Charlie smiled. 'Really.'

'I promise I'll keep very still, Charlie, really I will.'

Carrie laughed at her daughter's wide-eyed exuberance. 'Charlie's going to put some stuff into your cut to make it go all numb so you can't feel it when he sews it up. It'll sting a bit.'

'Like what the dentist put in Emmett's mouth?'

Charlie raised an eyebrow at Carrie and then looked back down at his patient. 'Who's Emmett? Is he your boyfriend?'

Dana giggled again. 'No, silly. He's my cousin. He's twelve and he had to have a filling 'cos he doesn't floss.'

Charlie smiled at Carrie again. 'Oh, dear. Do you floss?'

Dana nodded solemnly. 'Every night. Mummy makes me.'

Charlie laughed, totally charmed by Dana. 'That's what mummies are for.' He glanced at Carrie again and felt warm all over at the love and pleasure he saw in her eyes.

Carrie swallowed hard. Charlie was being so good with Dana. Their rapport had been instant from the night of the accident. She didn't need this man in her life. Making her crazy. Making her daughter laugh. Kissing her.

'OK, now, enough chatter. Hold my hand, Dana, and shut your eyes. Remember to stay very, very still. Squeeze Mummy's hand when it starts to sting. Squeeze it really hard. It'll be over soon and then you can go and have a dance.'

'OK, Mummy,' Dana said, shutting her eyes and screwing up her face.

Charlie smiled as he adjusted the position of Dana's chin. He nodded at Carrie. 'Ready?' he mouthed. Carrie nodded back and he could tell from the way she was holding Dana that she was ready to use her body to keep Dana still if she bucked.

Charlie inserted the fine needle into the edge of the wound. Dana flinched slightly but stayed still. But that was the easy part. Lignocaine stung like mad and he sent up a silent prayer that Dana would continue to be good. He slowly injected the local anaesthetic agent.

'Mummy?' Dana's eyes opened. 'It's hurting, Mummy.'

'It's OK, darling, squeeze my hand hard. It won't hurt for long,' Carrie said, rising and lying gently across Dana's body in case she tried to kick or twist. She could see tears shining in Dana's eyes and felt guilt and pride in equal measure. 'Mummy's giving you a special hug, see? You're being so brave, isn't she, Charlie?'

'Absolutely,' Charlie agreed. 'You're braver than a hundred boys. There…I've finished now.' He placed the syringe back on the trolley.

Dana sniffled. 'Really? You think I'm braver than a boy?'

Charlie chuckled. 'Definitely. Now we'll wait a couple of minutes for the local to make you numb then I'll sew you up, OK?'

'Then I get to dance?'

'I promise.'

Carrie listened absently to the lively conversation between Charlie and her daughter while they waited for the local to take effect. Charlie's regulation three-day growth and shaggy hair seemed even more endearing when he was talking to her child as if she was the most important thing in the world to him.

'Can you feel this?' Charlie asked Dana, giving her a light prick on the wound margin with the curved suture blade.

'No.'

'This?' Charlie asked again as he prodded several places.

'No.'

'OK, then. What colour button do you want me to use?'

Dana giggled. 'Charlie!'

Carrie smiled, too. 'OK, hold my hand again, darling. Won't be long now.'

Charlie maintained a patter of conversation as he placed four sutures in the wound, bringing the edges together. Dana was perfectly still, making his job much easier.

Carrie watched Charlie snip the last suture close to the skin. 'That looks great. Thank you, Charlie. Maybe your father is right?'

Charlie screwed up his nose. He doubted it. 'I'd rather watch paint dry. OK, Sleeping Beauty. Up you get. Your jukebox awaits.'

Charlie helped Dana up into a sitting position, her legs dangling over the edge again.

'What do you say to Charlie?' Carrie prompted.

'Thank you, thank you, thank you.' Dana grinned and then threw her arms around Charlie's neck and kissed him on the cheek.

Charlie sat stock still in the little girl's embrace. He glanced at Carrie, who was looking as stunned as he felt. For a moment he didn't know what he was supposed to do. He was shocked to register how good Dana's little arms felt clinging to his neck. And how sweet her skin smelt—like lollipops and sunshine.

'Sorry,' Carrie mouthed, remembering his fast exit from her house. He hadn't seemed particularly interested in kids then and he was looking at her with a look of apprehension and something else she couldn't quite make out.

'It's fine,' he mouthed back. How could anyone hold such sweet innocence in their arms and remain emotionally distant? Like his father had?

'Can I dance now?' Dana asked, dropping her arms.

'Sure,' he said, helping her down off the couch. He watched her walk out, her bunches bobbing, followed closely by

Carrie, her pinstriped hips swaying. What the hell was with these two females that in one week they had totally consumed him? One charmed him, the other exasperated him. Where the hell was his focus these days? He turned away from the doorway in disgust.

Ten minutes later he emerged to find Dana charming everyone in the waiting room with her jiggle. Not even the blood-stained T-shirt detracted from her cuteness. Even two big gruff male teenagers were grinning stupidly at her.

'She's a hit,' Charlie said, claiming the seat next to Carrie's on the double sofa.

Carrie laughed, trying to hide the sudden leap in her pulse as his thigh brushed against hers. 'Yes, quite the performer.'

They watched her for a few minutes in silence. 'I'd better get her home,' Carrie said, stirring. 'Could you keep an eye on her while I get my stuff together?'

'Sure,' Charlie agreed, not daring to look up at her and exceedingly grateful when she left.

Dana pirouetted and waved at Charlie. 'Can you dance with me, Charlie?'

Charlie groaned inwardly. Between the two Douglas women he didn't know whether he was Arthur or Martha. 'Sure, sweetie,' he said, rising from the couch and sweeping her off her feet, swinging her round while she giggled in delight.

'Here, step on my shoes,' he directed.

Dana did as she was told and he swirled her around the floor as she clung to his legs and laughed. She looked up at him with those big blue eyes and Charlie was utterly captivated.

Carrie came out and discovered them dancing and laughing together and felt her pulse slow, the music fade away and her vision telescope. They could have been father and daughter. Wasn't that what fathers did with their daughters? Let them stand on their feet and dance with them? That's what her father had done. Damn Rupert, damn him for denying Dana such simple pleasures. Such precious memories.

'Mummy! I'm dancing with Charlie.'

Charlie stumbled slightly when he realised they were being watched by Carrie. Their gazes locked and he could see the yearning in Carrie's gaze.

'So you are, darling,' Carrie said, finding her voice.

'Your turn to dance with Charlie,' Dana pronounced, breaking away and running over to clutch at her mother's hand and drag her towards Charlie.

'Oh… I… No, darling. I'm sure Charlie doesn't want to dance with Mummy.' Carrie resisted the pull on her hand.

Like hell Charlie doesn't.

'Oh, please, Mummy. Please, please.'

'Sweetheart, you know Mummy's not a very good dancer,' Carrie said.

'He'll let you stand on his feet, won't you, Charlie?'

Carrie gave a nervous laugh. 'Darling, I'm too heavy for Charlie, I'll break his toes.'

Charlie thought how great her weight had felt against him the other night. Pushed against him. Rubbing against him. He felt a rise of naked heat. A surge of potent desire. 'Nonsense,' he said, grabbing Carrie's hand and twirling her towards him as 'Rock Around the Clock' blared out.

Carrie spun crazily and landed against Charlie's hard body for one cataclysmic second before he pushed her out again, spinning her away from him. He spun her around and twisted and jived, their hands linked, her heart hammering madly. Dana sat on the lounge and clapped excitedly. One of the teenagers wolf-whistled. By the time the music stopped and Elvis was crooning 'Love Me Tender', Carrie's entire world was spinning.

'Me, oh, me.' Dana jumped up excitedly. 'Let's all dance together.'

Carrie nodded as Charlie released her and took Dana's hand. She looked down to see her daughter had also commandeered Charlie's hand.

'Mummy, this is the song from the wedding last week.'

Carrie shook her head, trying to clear her hazy thought processes. Her cells still rocking around the clock. 'Oh, yes, it was the wedding waltz.'

'Waltz with me, Mummy, like you did with Grandpa at the wedding.'

Carrie smiled down at her beguiling little girl, finding her as hard to resist as ever. Even the suture line gave her a certain appeal. She hauled Dana up onto her hip.

'Charlie, too,' Dana said, hooking an arm around Charlie's neck and drawing them into an intimate circle.

Carrie daren't look at him as Charlie's arm slid around her back. She could hear his breathing and was excruciatingly conscious of the sheer male presence of him. From his spicy aftershave to his reassuring bulk.

This was wrong. It was too intimate. Not in the way it had been on Friday night. But intimate in the way a family was intimate. And it felt so good for something so wrong. This was a family of two. It was pointless thinking otherwise. Or getting Dana too caught up in it. But it was so nice she found it hard to step away, despite the dictates of her very sensible brain.

The song came to an end and Charlie stepped away abruptly. For a crazy second there he had felt more like part of a family then he had during his entire childhood. Dana had moved Carrie and himself into dangerous territory with the memory of their passion still so vivid.

Carrie looked up at his sudden withdrawal. She was again reminded of his quick-as-a-flash departure the other night. Why did a man who was so good with kids run a mile from them? Obviously being nice to a child and wanting one were two different things.

'We'd better go,' she said quietly, not wanting to face rejection again, not with Dana involved, too. She kissed the top of her daughter's head. 'Say good bye to Charlie, sweetheart.'

Dana waggled her fingers at him. 'Bye, Charlie. Can I come and dance to your dukebox again?'

Charlie laughed and flicked one of her bunches. 'Any time, Sleeping Beauty.'

Charlie stood in the middle of the lounge area, watching them walk away ignoring the heavy feeling in the vicinity of his heart. Maybe there was something to this commitment thing after all?

CHAPTER FIVE

THE week ground by with snail-like slowness. Carrie was there, a constant presence in his staffroom, hanging around, pestering him for figures while hers drove him crazy in those pinstripe suits. Joe popped in and out with annoying frequency, making banal observations and counting down the days. Angela ruled the place with an iron fist. The jukebox thumped. Kids came and went. Stressed-out parents came and went. Police came and went.

When Friday finally came around Charlie welcomed the day with mixed feelings. It was hard to believe that it had been a year to the day that an HIV-positive drug addict had deliberately stabbed him with an infected needle. And that today was the day of his blood test. His final blood test.

It didn't seem to matter that all the others over the past year had been clear and it was against all the odds for this one to come back positive—the possibility was still there. What if it was positive? What if he had to shift from maybe having the disease to actually having the disease? OK, the stats were on his side and it wasn't the death sentence that it had been with the medication they now had but still...

It was a mental barrier that he hadn't been able to get past. He'd been putting his life on hold for this moment. He'd shelved his expansion plans for the centre, denied himself a sex life and buried himself within these four walls from early morning to late at night. He'd lurched from his separation to his divorce to his health crisis and consequently work had been his solace for over three years. What the hell was he going to do if he didn't have to do that any more?

'Today's the day,' Joe said, interrupting Charlie's thoughts and dumping the regulation cup of coffee in front of him on his desk. 'What time's your appointment?'

'I'm ducking out at lunch.'

'And then it's how long…?'

'Should get them back mid next week.'

'Then we're hitting the town? Right?'

Charlie nodded unenthusiastically. 'Right.'

Joe's brow furrowed. He was getting worried about Charlie. A year of celibacy had really messed up his mind. He'd become a workaholic hermit. The last few years Charlie had been all work, work, work.

It wasn't even seven o'clock yet and he was at his desk. 'The Mill is jumping midweek.'

'OK, sure,' Charlie agreed tonelessly, sipping his coffee.

Joe shook his head and laughed. 'Don't worry, old mate. We'll get you hooked up and this whole nightmare will be behind you. You'll be able to get on with your life. It'll be like it never happened.'

Oh, no. One thing was for sure. This was one thing he was never going to forget had happened. 'I think I've forgotten how to pick up women, Joe.' Had he forgotten or was it just so completely uninteresting to him now? Facing death had given him pause to review his life.

Joe cracked up. 'You?' He laughed. 'Impossible. Even a wedding ring didn't deter women. All you have to do is just sit back and let it happen.'

A few weeks ago he'd been champing at the bit to release a year's worth of pent-up frustration but on D-day it now didn't seem so important. The thought of picking up a stranger and taking her home left him cold. The only woman that pre-occupied him these days was the one who sat in his staffroom all day with a bunch of figures and a pair of lips he was supposed to be forgetting about.

He took another sip of coffee. It was official—he had a thing for Dr Carrie Douglas.

Carrie arrived at work shortly after seven. She was hoping a few early starts would help her complete her investigation sooner. Even if it was just a day or two. That was one advantage of having a live-in nanny!

She placed the key she'd insisted Charlie provide for her in the front door, only to discover the centre all ready open. No clients were in yet but she could hear the murmur of voices from Charlie's office.

'Hi,' she called, smiling at Joe and nodding to Charlie as she walked past his open door.

She ignored the flare of heat she'd seen in Charlie's steady grey gaze. The same flare she'd seen that night they were supposed to be forgetting about. Heavens, how was she going to get through another fortnight of this insanity?

Her attraction to Charlie was getting harder and harder to ignore. Even at home, away from the centre, she was getting no respite—Dana made sure of that. Charlie was her newest favourite person and she hadn't stopped chattering about him. Or his damn dukebox.

She was setting up her laptop when he waltzed into the staffroom.

'How's Dana?' he asked, fixing himself another coffee.

Carrie gritted her teeth. The mutual admiration society was wearing thin. 'Fine.'

'Those sutures can come out at the weekend.' He stirred his drink.

'Yes, thank you, Charlie. I can count to five.' She clicked on her file.

Charlie turned and raised an eyebrow at her as he leant back against the sink. 'You can bring her in and I'll take them out if you want.'

Did he not think her capable? 'I know you don't have a whole lot of faith in my doctoring skills, Charlie, but I'm pretty sure even I can manage to remove four sutures.'

What the hell? Something had put her knickers well and truly in a twist. *No. Do not think about her knickers!* 'I know.' He shrugged, sipping at his drink. 'I just thought, you know…I'm going to be here anyway, and I thought she might enjoy another dance.' He smiled, thinking about Dana's dance style.

'You're going to be here?'

He nodded.

'So, let me get this straight.' She looked at him over her glasses. 'You're here at the crack of dawn until late at night. And weekends? Charlie, I hate to break this to you but you need a life.'

This from a woman who pretended she'd rather deal with piles of paperwork than minister to the sick and needy, a role to which she was so obviously suited. 'You sound like Joe.'

She nodded and returned to her work. 'I knew I liked Joe for a reason.'

Hearing her talk affectionately about his friend churned in his gut. 'So, that's a no to me removing the sutures?'

She gave him a you're-interrupting-me look. 'Yes. That's a no. Look, thanks, but even if I wasn't doing it myself, I hardly think this is the place for a kid to hang out.'

He felt another twist in his gut. She sounded just like Veronica. She looked untouchable again in her pinstripes and glasses. 'But it was OK in an emergency?'

She heard the steel in his voice and saw his eyes turn icy. 'I'm sorry,' she said, taking her glasses off. 'I didn't mean to offend you. But you've got to concede I'm right. This place isn't exactly Buckingham Palace. She's four. Call me over-protective but I'd like to shelter her from this side of life for as long as I can.'

He straightened. He was so used to his colourful working environment he often didn't see the grungy aspect. But he supposed that mothers had to worry about that type of thing. What the hell did he know about being a parent? 'Of course, you're right. I'll let you get back to your work.'

Carrie watched as the door shut behind him. The end of her assignment couldn't come soon enough.

Charlie sat in the chair while an efficient-looking woman with a severe hairdo and a twinkle in her eye extracted blood from the vein in the crook of his elbow.

'Last one, love?' she asked.

Charlie nodded. 'Sure is, Liz.'

'At least you'll be able to get on with your life now, love,' she chatted away.

Charlie nodded again. Liz was the second person to utter those words today. How many times had he thought them this last year? Getting the all-clear so he could bring his life off hold? Carrie's words from earlier taunted him—*you need a life*.

He watched his blood pour into the blood tube. Infected by a deadly virus? Or not? A flip of a card. A roll of a dice. Is this what his life had become? *You need a life.* The words reverberated around his head. Liz unclipped the tourniquet and stuck some gauze at the puncture site.

'Bend your arm up,' she instructed unnecessarily.

Charlie did as he was told. *You need a life.*

'Just a few more days now, Charlie.'

He stared at Liz.

You need a life.

Just a few more days now.

Did he really want to wait a few more days? He'd waited for three hundred and sixty-five of them. More, if he counted the numerous blurry years as his marriage had disintegrated and the divorce became final.

Did he want to waste one single day more? Suddenly everything crystallised in his head. He grabbed Liz by the shoulders and gave her a huge peck on the cheek.

'No, Liz, today. Right now, today.'

He kissed her cheek again and practically sprinted out of the pathology clinic. He'd been feeling sorry for himself for an entire year. Putting everything on hold just in case. In case what? He had HIV? So what if he did? Was he just going to give up work? Take to his bed and wait to die? When he could have decades to live? Decades to make a difference?

Well, no more. Carrie had challenged him to get a life and that was exactly what he was going to do. Well…more of a life anyway. Starting right now. His brisk long-legged stride had him back at the drop-in centre within minutes.

He inspected the outside with a critical eye. It was looking old and worn, even though it had only opened five years ago. He'd been too busy keeping it running to notice how drab it looked and there was never enough money for luxuries such as paint anyway. That was about to change.

Charlie strode through the front door, ignoring Angela's cheery hello. He headed for his office, opening the filing cabinet, found the 'E' section and flicked through until he found the expansion plans for the drop-in centre. He shook his head at his complacency—he should have filed them under 'P' for prat.

He left his office and marched to the staffroom with a single-minded determination he hadn't felt since before his marriage had fallen apart. He crashed the door open and stood staring at a startled Carrie.

'Charlie?'

'I have something to show you.'

Carrie watched him move towards her, carrying a long roll of paper in his hand. She noticed the gauze at the crook of his elbow as he drew closer. Pills and now blood tests? Or maybe he'd given a blood donation? 'I'm kind of busy…'

'Oh, you're going to want to see this.' Charlie pushed some coffee-cups aside and laid the plans out flat in the middle of the table. He placed a mug on each corner.

Carrie recognised architectural drawings when she saw them. But of what? She sighed and removed her glasses. 'Building a house?'

Charlie laughed, leaning over the plans and admiring them again for the first time in a year. 'Better. I'm remodelling the centre.'

Carrie stared at the plans. Was he mad? The centre was going under—big time. 'These are…adventurous.'

He nodded. 'Yes.' Charlie straightened and pushed away from the table. He moved to the sink and flicked on the kettle. 'For five years I've struggled to keep everything going on a shoestring budget. Offering limited services in an area that's crying out for maximum support. And it's not good enough. This idea…' he walked back to the table, leant over and poked a finger at his plans '…addresses all the areas that are sadly lacking at the moment.'

He pushed away again and paced back and forth, aware she was analysing the plans. He ran his hand through his hair. 'I want to be able to provide full-time legal advice and have a full-time counsellor. I want to be able to run a needle exchange and a methadone programme and have another doctor or two so we can really provide a top-notch service.'

He walked back to the table and braced his hands on the back of a chair. 'I want this to be a one-stop shop to meet all this community's needs.'

Carrie stared at him, moved by the passion in his voice. By

the excitement that was evident in every bodily nuance. He obviously cared for this community enormously. He looked invigorated and very, very committed. His grey gaze was earnest. She'd never seen him looking sexier.

But she wasn't paid to be swept away by passionate ideals, even if they were being delivered so eloquently by a man who had pushed her against a door and kissed her breath away.

'And where will the money come from?'

'The bottom line again, Carrie?'

She heard the disdain in his voice and saw the contemptuous curl of his lips. 'Yes, Charlie, The bottom line. Sorry to be so boring but a project of this magnitude…' she tapped the plans with a pen '…takes serious cash.' She didn't have the heart to tell him that her investigation would probably lead to a recommendation of closure.

'Once you've finished your financial analysis I'll take everything to the hospital board. The plans and my ideas on funding them. This kind of project should attract a lot of monetary support from government, private and community sources.'

'I don't know, Charlie,' Carrie said, her gaze returning to the plans. She chose her words carefully. 'The drop-in centre is hardly a financial gold mine to start with. This will be a really hard sell.'

Charlie pushed away from the chair. 'It's a free clinic, Carrie. It's not in our charter to make a profit.'

'It's not in your charter to lose money, either. If you do succeed in convincing them to do this, you're going to need to keep your books better.'

Charlie grinned at her. 'I'll put a part-time bookkeeper in my proposal.'

Carrie shook her head as she watched him swagger out the door.

* * *

Charlie attacked the rest of the day with renewed vigour. He felt like he was starting afresh. The excitement he'd felt when he'd first had the plans drawn up returned. Formulating them shortly after his separation from Veronica had taken his mind off what had been happening in his personal life and he had worked on them day and night. Then a year ago his whole life had changed again in the blink of an eye, and he had put everything on hold. But no more. He intended to take his life back. No matter what it held.

An hour after Angela left for the day Charlie was at the front desk, looking for a file, when a young woman staggered into the clinic. She looked about seventeen and was clutching the two edges of her torn T-shirt together, one breast half-exposed. Her skirt was ripped, her face red and bruised, her bottom lip swollen and bleeding. She was sobbing and her mascara had run all down her face.

Charlie raced around the other side of the desk and caught her before she collapsed.

'Don't touch me, don't touch me,' she screamed at Charlie, struggling to free herself from his hold.

Charlie released her instantly. Everyone in the lounge and waiting area stopped and stared, the jukebox the only noise.

The girl didn't look familiar to Charlie. 'It's OK. I'm a doctor. My name's Charlie. You look hurt. What happened?'

The girl looked at him with fear and rage in her eyes. 'I couldn't stop him, he was too big.'

Charlie felt a sinking feeling in the pit of his stomach. The girl had been raped. Damn it, he needed Angela! 'Jordan,' he said to the nearest open-mouthed teenager, 'go and get Carrie.'

Jordan scuttled past quickly and hurried down the hallway to the staffroom.

'It's OK,' Charlie said again to the frightened girl, 'No one's going to hurt you here. You're safe now.'

Carrie strode briskly down the hallway, Jordan close behind. She arrived on the scene and stifled a horrified gasp at the badly beaten girl with wild eyes, her stance wary and agitated.

'This is Carrie,' Charlie said quietly. 'She's a doctor, too.'

Carrie felt the denial rise to her lips. No, no, no. She wasn't here for this. Ever since she'd met Charlie he'd been dragging her into situations she didn't want to be in. Had given up before Dana's birth. But the wounded-animal look in the girl's eyes called to something deep inside her, and she just couldn't turn away from such a wretched soul.

'How about you go with her and she sees to your injuries?'

Carrie looked at Charlie. The look in his eyes was almost as desperate as the girl's. He needed her to do this for him, for this girl. But more than that, his slight nod told her he had faith in her. That she could do it. That she'd be OK.

Carrie took a deep breath and took a hesitant step towards the frightened girl, giving her a reassuring smile. 'Hi,' she said. 'Why don't we go in there?' She pointed behind her to the treatment room. 'Then I'll clean up your face.'

The girl swung her gaze from Charlie to Carrie. 'I tried to stop him.'

'I know,' Carrie said gently, holding out her hand. 'Come on, you're safe now.'

The girl looked at Carrie's hand and then back at Charlie and then back at Carrie. 'I don't want him,' she said to Carrie, pointing at Charlie.

Carrie flicked a glance at Charlie. *I do.* At the moment she wanted his back-up and support more than anything. 'No, it's OK, just you and me. Just the two of us.'

The girl wavered for a moment and then nodded, walking warily towards Carrie. Carrie put her arm around the girl's shoulders. She felt her flinch slightly. 'It's OK. Come on, not far.' She led the girl to the treatment room, helped her up onto the examination table and turned to shut the door.

'Find her some clothes,' she said to Charlie, who was hovering outside.

He nodded. 'I'll give you a plastic bag to put her other clothes in. The police will want them for evidence. Wear gloves. I'll get a counsellor from the rape crisis centre over and call the police.'

Carrie nodded and shut the door. She took a deep breath before she turned around to face the girl again. She'd had no experience with sexual assault victims.

She opened some cupboards against the far wall, looking for a dressing pack of some description to clean the girl's cut lip. It also gave her time to think of how she was going to deal with the situation. To say she felt out of her depth was an understatement.

Carrie found what she needed and fussed over opening the pack and pouring some antiseptic liquid into one of the plastic pots. She placed it on the trolley and pushed it over, dragging the mobile stool as she went.

'What's your name?' Carrie asked as she sat on the stool, the long-forgotten clinician inside her assessing the girl's battered face.

'R-Roberta,' she said, her arms crossed across her torn T-shirt.

'Hi, Roberta.' Carrie reached down and pulled some gloves out of a box on the bottom of the trolley. 'Would you like to get out of those clothes?'

Roberta looked down at her tattered and bloodied clothes and nodded her head.

'I'll have to bag them for the police, is that OK?'

'The police?'

Carrie saw Roberta recoil. 'Yes. You do want this man caught, don't you?'

Carrie saw a host of emotions flit across Roberta's broken

face and feared that the girl was about to burst into tears. Then a hardness entered her eyes and her jaw clenched. 'I want him to rot in a jail cell for ever.'

There was a quiet knock at the door and Roberta startled clutching at Carrie's arm. Carrie covered Roberta's hand with hers. 'It's OK. It'll be Charlie with some new clothes.'

Roberta's grip eased and she nodded at Carrie.

Carrie rose and opened the door. 'Thanks,' she said to Charlie, accepting the bundle he gave her.

'How's it going?'

'OK…I think.'

Charlie nodded. 'The counsellor and the cops should be here soon.'

'Thanks.' Carrie closed the door and went back to tend to Roberta.

Roberta winced as Carrie touched some gauze to her shattered lip. 'Sorry,' she murmured.

'Bastard punched me in the face. Twice. What gave him the right to do this?' Roberta demanded. 'Because I'm a hooker to put food in my kid's mouth? I told him I was off duty but he wouldn't take no for an answer.'

Roberta started to cry and Carrie felt helpless. Anger and revulsion raged inside her at the ordeal this girl had been through.

'Do you remember what he looked like? Do you know him?'

Roberta sniffled. 'I've seen him around. But what's the point? They're never going to believe a hooker crying wolf.'

Carrie didn't know much about these things but a blind man could see that Roberta had been assaulted. 'Let me feel your face,' Carrie said, putting down the gauze now the lip had been attended to. 'Tell me where it hurts.'

'It hurts everywhere,' Roberta said.

Carrie prodded gently around Roberta's facial bones, looking for asymmetry and feeling for any obvious malformations or any signs of crepitis—bone rubbing against bone.

There didn't appear to be any teeth broken and her bite seemed reasonably aligned.

'Think you'll need an X-ray just to check you don't have any fractures.'

Roberta nodded. 'Can I get dressed?'

'Sure,' Carrie said, pulling the mobile screen in place and handing her the clean clothes. 'Just put your other clothes on the bed and I'll bag them.'

'All I want is a shower,' Roberta said from behind the screen. 'I can smell him everywhere.'

'I know, but it's best if we collect the evidence from your body for the police first.'

'I'm done,' Roberta said a minute later.

Carrie pulled back the screen and helped Roberta back onto the table. She was gathering her discarded clothes together when there was another knock on the door.

Carrie opened it. There was an older woman standing with Charlie. She looked to be in her forties, her tough exterior betrayed by her friendly eyes. 'Carrie, this is Rene Chalk. She's from the rape crisis centre.'

Carrie smiled at the newcomer. 'Come in,' she invited.

Charlie performed the introductions and Carrie prepared to leave. 'No, don't go.' Roberta demanded, her voice rising. 'I want you to stay.'

Carrie looked at Charlie, surprised and startled by Roberta's request. Charlie nodded. So did Rene. So Carrie stayed and listened to Rene talk things over with Roberta. They talked a little about the assault but mainly about what would happen next. The police and court proceedings. Rene offered and urged Roberta to seek free counselling at the rape crisis centre in the next few days and to continue it for as long as she felt she needed it.

The police were next. Roberta was adamant that she didn't want Charlie collecting the rape evidence so Carrie performed that, too, in the presence of Rene and a female police officer, who bagged the evidence as Carrie collected it. The officer also took photos of the facial injuries and the bruising on Roberta's thighs.

Two hours later Carrie was emotionally exhausted but also strangely elated. Roberta's reliance on her had made her feel as if she'd actually made a difference to someone's life again. And she hadn't had that feeling for a long time. It was why she'd become a doctor in the first place. What she'd once thrived on. She hadn't realised how much she'd missed it. Until now.

Rene had left with Roberta accompanying her to the police station to make a formal statement and then to the hospital for X-rays. Charlie was in his office, dealing with all the paperwork.

Carrie wandered down to the staffroom. It was after five and she really needed to get home. Now the crisis was over she felt strangely depleted and she sat at the table for a moment to collect herself, staring at her laptop—another wasted afternoon.

Carrie sighed. She was never going to get this finished. And she really, really needed to because the longer she was around Charlie the more she began to question the direction of her life. And she was very comfortable with that direction. Or at least she had been.

The door opened. 'Well, that's the paperwork done. Thanks so much for earlier, Carrie. You were wonderful,' Charlie said, walking straight to the table and sitting down.

Do not listen to his praise. You are on track to becoming Australia's youngest MD. 'Didn't really have a whole lot of choice, did I?'

'That's why we need the expansion.' Charlie winked. 'A female doctor around here would be very handy.'

Carrie shook her head. 'You know there's no way the board is going to agree to your plans.'

He shrugged. 'I'm feeling suddenly optimistic.'

She shook her head again. He was smiling at her and his grey eyes, three-day growth and shaggy hair oozed sex appeal.

'Well, don't count your chickens,' she warned wearily, packing up her stuff.

'Nothing ventured, nothing gained.' He watched her zipping her laptop away. 'What about you?'

'What about me?'

'Well, I made a decision today to get my life back on track. To stop treading water and get back in there again. But what about you? Today you demonstrated yet again how good a clinician you are. Isn't it time you gave up all this—' he picked up some of her papers and threw them in the air '—and got back to what you're really good at?'

Carrie watched the papers float down, some landing on the table, the others on the floor. She glared at him. 'They were in order,' she snapped.

'Good,' he said firmly. 'Stop hiding behind them, Carrie.'

Carrie gritted her teeth and collected the scattered papers. Her heart hammered as she bit back a hundred things she wanted to say. She jammed them in her briefcase. 'What I do with my life is none of your business.'

Charlie shook his head. 'You're wasting your talent.'

'Guess you know how your father feels now,' she snapped, sweeping her briefcase off the table, ripping her jacket off the back of her chair and stalking out of the room, slamming the door behind her for good measure.

Charlie sat at the table unmoving for a few moments. *Touché, Carrie. Touché.*

CHAPTER SIX

CARRIE arrived at the centre on Wednesday morning and was surprised not to see Charlie sitting at his desk. Surely she hadn't beaten him in? They'd barely spoken since his comment on Friday, trading polite, brief conversation only.

She opened the door to the staffroom to find him sitting at the table, turning an envelope over and over in his hands. His usual mug was in front of him.

'Morning.'

Charlie looked up from the yellow envelope that contained his test results. For once her pinstriped primness didn't register. 'Morning.'

'Would you like a refill?' she asked politely, switching the kettle on.

Charlie tapped the envelope against the wood of the table. 'Yes, please.' He drank the cold dregs of his current cup and held it out for her to take.

Carrie put her laptop on the table and took the mug. She put coffee into both the cups, aware of his brooding presence behind her, and poured the boiling water, adding sugar and milk to his and milk only to hers. She carried them over to the table, plonking his down and taking a seat herself. Charlie was still staring at the envelope.

Carrie blew on the hot liquid and took a sip. 'Worried it's a letter bomb?'

Charlie gave a grudging smile. 'What's in here is potentially explosive.' It could potentially detonate his whole life.

'Looks official,' she commented. The envelope looked just like the generic yellow ones they used in most government organisations.

Charlie nodded. 'It is.'

Carrie took another sip. 'So…you're just going to look at it?'

Charlie threw the envelope on the table. 'They're my test results.'

She nodded. So he hadn't given blood the other day. 'From the blood test you had on Friday?'

'You're very observant.'

Carrie smiled. 'I have a four-year-old. You have to be on the ball.'

He chuckled. 'Yeah, I bet Dana keeps you on your toes.'

'That she does.'

A few more moments passed where they both sipped at their coffee and stared at the envelope. It was hard to believe that a piece of yellow paper could be so compelling.

Carrie glanced at him. What was he waiting for? Obviously whatever was in that envelope was big for Charlie. Just what exactly did he have? 'Are you sick?'

Charlie tore his gaze from the centre of the table. 'I hope not.' He picked the envelope up and stared at the address label. He couldn't explain why he was reluctant to open it. A year of his life had been focused solely on what was inside this envelope.

He glanced up at Carrie. She was looking at him expectantly. Waiting for him to elaborate. What the hell—he'd do anything to delay opening the envelope.

'A year ago I was pricked with a used syringe by an HIV-positive drug addict.'

Carrie gaped. She certainly hadn't been expecting that. A

familial disease maybe, hell, even cancer. But HIV? 'Oh, no, how awful. How did that happen? Was it left in the clinic somewhere?'

Carrie knew that needle-stick injuries were an occupational hazard and that even the most careful practitioners could fall victim.

'No. It was a deliberate attack here, late one night. It was Donny.'

Deliberate? 'Donny? Tilly's uncle?'

Charlie nodded. 'He came in late one night armed with a used syringe and demanded my wallet.'

Her eyes grew wider. 'So you fought with him?'

'No, I gave him my money. I only had twenty bucks. He became enraged because it was nowhere near enough and lashed out with the syringe and buried it in my arm.'

Carrie listened, wide-eyed, not really able to comprehend what Charlie must have been through. 'But Donny seemed fine to me.'

Charlie nodded. 'He is. Now. I know it's hard to believe but he was addicted to heroin for many years. The incident with me was the catalyst for him to get clean. His rock bottom, I suppose you can say. He's off the stuff now and is training to be a youth worker. I'd love to be able to employ him when the expansion goes ahead.'

Carrie ignored the reference to the expansion. 'That's very forgiving of you.'

He shrugged. 'Drugs mess with your head. They turn you into someone that you're not. Was I angry with Donny that he jeopardised my health? Yes. Do I blame him? No. The Donny who stabbed me a year ago is not the man he is now. Kicking the habit is hard. Very, very hard—but he did it. He got clean. And his remorse is strong.'

Carrie nodded slowly, remembering the hushed conversation she'd overheard between the two men the night Donny had brought the overdose case to the clinic. Donny's concern about Charlie's medication.

Still, it took an enormous amount of human decency to turn the other cheek. 'So you've been living under this cloud ever since.' Things were starting to fall in place for her now. The medication he took and how he had double-gloved when suturing Dana's chin. It hadn't been to protect him from anything she might have had but the other way round.

'Yes.' He nodded.

Carrie searched back through her memory. It was amazing how much knowledge became rusty when it wasn't being used every day. 'I would imagine your risk of contracting HIV was very low, though.'

'Yes, ordinarily transmission rates are much lower than those of say hep B, which miraculously he didn't have. But Donny was completely non-compliant with his HIV meds and would have had a very high viral load. The occupational health team recommended I take the prophylactic triple cocktail.'

'The meds I've seen you take are antiretrovirals?'

He nodded. 'My HIV antibody tests at three and six months were both negative.'

Carrie felt the knot in her stomach loosen a little. 'Surely that puts you in the clear?'

'I've read of rare cases where the window has extended beyond six months. The occupational health people erred on the side of caution, too, and have kept me covered for the full year.'

'And that's your twelve-month result?' Carrie nodded at the envelope.

Charlie nodded. 'I know that the chances of it being positive are near to impossible but I have the feeling I'm holding my whole life in my hands and I just can't bring myself to open it.'

Carrie felt his torment. Four years ago she'd had a similar letter that had held her whole future in it, too. She hadn't been able to open it at all for fear of what it held.

His uncertainty appealed to her, her insides melting at his hesitancy. She was used to seeing him in command, in control. From the car accident the night they'd first met, to the OD, to her car being vandalised, to Dana's sutures, to Roberta and his expansion plans. He was a take-charge kind of guy.

She felt strangely compelled to share her own experience. Let him know that sometimes life railroaded you and all you could do was hang on. That you couldn't take charge of everything—sometimes circumstances took charge instead. Anything to put that teasing sparkle back in his worried grey gaze.

'I know how you feel.'

Charlie glanced at her. 'Oh, yeah?'

'I had an official-looking letter like that four years ago, just after Dana was born. It held the results of the Medical Registration Board's review into an incident I was involved in where a child died.'

Carrie held her breath. She'd never talked about the horrible incident to anyone other than her family. In fact, she hadn't talked about it in a long time at all, just buried it and the churning emotions that usually overwhelmed her beneath mounds of paper.

Charlie noted the rigid way Carrie was holding her cup, the way her gaze didn't quite meet his. This was obviously difficult for her to talk to about. It also explained a lot. He'd suspected all along something serious had occurred in her career.

'What happened?' he asked gently.

Carrie's hand shook. Rehashing that awful night didn't seem quite so easy now.

'It's OK,' he said, and reached out a hand to cover hers. 'You don't have to tell me.'

She saw the compassion in his eyes, the softening, his reassuring smile. Suddenly she wanted to tell him more than anything. To talk to someone who knew how crazy it could be at the coalface. Who could relate. Empathise even. Family understood because they loved you. Colleagues understood because they'd lived it.

She stared into the murky depths of her coffee. 'I was an intern working in Accident and Emergency. It was one of those crazy Saturday nights where half of Brisbane seemed to either have food poisoning or flu. And it was full of the usual bloodied drunks and we had a major car accident that had just come in, along with a fractured neck of femur from a nursing home. It was mad.' She looked up from her coffee. 'Bit like here, really.'

Charlie chuckled and it was such a lovely warm noise it gave her the courage to continue.

'A man bought in a friend's child who he was minding for a few hours, complaining that the child had bad breath and he'd rung the mother and she'd told him to bring the boy into us.'

Charlie cringed—halitosis in a busy emergency department. That must have gone down like a lead balloon. 'I gather the child wasn't assessed as a priority.'

Carrie gave a small smile and shook her head. 'So after an hour of waiting he starts to get annoyed and there was a bit of a lull amidst all the chaos so the nurses asked if I would see the little boy next.'

'And you did?'

Carrie nodded. 'Kind of. The chart was handed to me, I called the boy's name—his name was Harry, Harry Pengelly…' As long as she lived she would never, ever forget the boy's name or his face.

Charlie heard her voice go husky as she mentioned the patient's name. No wonder she hadn't been able to function properly at the accident scene. This obviously still affected her very badly.

'I didn't open the chart. I asked what the problem was. He said, "The kid's mouth stinks like an animal's died back there." And he was right, it did smell very offensive. I asked some basic questions—had he eaten anything unusual or different, had he choked on anything and about his medical history of which this guy knew nothing. At a quick glance the child seemed reasonably alert, a little pale but he was interactive and certainly didn't appear unwell. So I said to wait there, I was going to get some equipment to look down Harry's throat.

'I left to get a tongue depressor and a torch and planned on doing a more complete assessment once I'd established he didn't have a visible obstruction. I was stopped twice by nursing staff for different medical orders so it was probably ten minutes before I got back to the cubicle, but by then the man had gone and taken Harry with him.'

Charlie nodded. Too often people grew impatient at the wait and left emergency departments without being seen.

'The triage nurse said he'd stormed out, muttering about incompetence. I planned to flip through the boy's chart but a middle-aged man with a suspected heart attack came through the doors and the chart got left on the doctors' desk.'

'I'm getting a sense that there was some significant medical history with Harry.'

Carrie nodded, tears pricking her eyes. She blinked rapidly. She hadn't cried over this in a long time and she wasn't going to start again in front of Charlie.

'Two hours later a woman runs into the department, an unconscious Harry in her arms. It was his mother. She was crying hysterically. He was cold, shocked, shut down. Unresponsive. Whiter than a sheet. His abdo was distended. We rushed him into Resus. Mum was too emotional to put a sentence together and someone grabbed his chart and flipped it open and discovered that he was ten days post-adenoid and tonsillectomy.'

Charlie shut his eyes. 'He'd had a bleed?'

Carrie nodded. 'Massive. No sooner had we discovered this than he vomited, and it was just all blood, some old, a lot fresh.

There was so much of it and it was so red against these white, white sheets, and it covered his pale floppy body like a river.' Carrie shuddered. 'I had nightmares for a year about the blood.'

Charlie remembered the way she had looked at the blood pumping out of the road-accident victim and her behaviour suddenly made sense. He cringed, thinking how insistent he'd been.

'We cannulated him, filled him with fluid and rushed him to Theatre to locate the source of the bleed and have it cauterised, but it was too late. He arrested on the table. The coroner found that Harry's operative site had probably been trickling for days and he'd been swallowing it and had presented the second time in irreversible hypovolaemic shock.'

Charlie felt for Carrie. She'd been through an awful experience. No wonder her faith in herself as a practitioner was permanently dented. 'And because you were the doctor who saw him that night, you carried the can? That's rough.'

Carrie nodded. 'I was suspended immediately pending an internal hospital review. That's when I inherited my desk job. The medical director was delighted to have someone with a business degree around. The review found I had no case to answer but it was automatically referred to the Registration Board so I was kept on suspension from clinical duties pending that decision.

'And to be perfectly honest, I was mess. I was so upset about that poor little boy and stressed out by the enormity of it all, it played havoc with my body. I lost weight, I couldn't sleep and when I did I had nightmares.'

Charlie could tell by the haunted look in her eyes that she'd been through the mill. 'I hope you received counselling.'

'Yes, and it helped but then I discovered I was pregnant. And Rupert, Dana's father, who hadn't been very supportive during the whole process at all, dropped me like a hot cake.'

Charlie shook his head in amazement. 'Nice.'

'Oh, yeah, just what I needed. And as D-day approached the more panicky I became. I didn't want to be struck off or have any further disciplinary action taken against me, but the thought of going back to clinical practice scared me more. I felt like I was in limbo.'

Charlie nodded. That was a very apt description. Limbo. Waiting for the elevator ride up or down.

'So when my letter arrived I couldn't bring myself to open it, either. I mean, I'd put my whole life on hold waiting for the damn thing but when it arrived I was too scared to open it.'

'But you did, right?'

Carrie shook her head. 'After looking at it for five hours, I got into my car and drove 'round to my sister's shop and got her to open it.'

Charlie stared at her, trying to fathom how truthful she was being. She looked embarrassed, sitting there chewing her lip, and he laughed out loud. 'You really did, didn't you?'

'Yep.' She nodded. 'I really did.'

'And it was good news?'

'They agreed with the hospital review and my suspension was lifted immediately. But by then I knew I couldn't ever go back. Even now, I still see his face, have nightmares about the blood. Not as much as in the beginning, but it's still affecting me.'

Which was a travesty. The glimpses he'd seen of her clinical side screamed of her competence. Even that night on the road, her professional instincts had shown through despite the demons she'd battled in her head. The way she'd applied pressure to the pumping artery had been one hundred per cent professional.

They both stared into their coffee, lost in their own thoughts for a minute.

Charlie came to a decision. 'You open it for me.' He picked up the envelope and held it out to her.

Carrie looked at him and the envelope then back at him. The denial that rose inside her died on her lips. He was serious. His grey gaze was steady, unflinching.

'Come on.' He grinned. 'Pretend you're my sister.'

If only. At least this insane attraction she felt for him wouldn't be an issue. Her hand shook slightly as she accepted the envelope. Carrie removed the letter-opener from her laptop bag and slit the envelope open. She pulled the path form out and scanned it briefly.

'Negative.' She smiled, turning it around to show him.

Charlie didn't do anything for a few seconds as the news sank in. *Negative. Negative. Negative.* It echoed around his brain. 'Negative.' He smiled back at Carrie.

She nodded and then laughed as the smile on his face grew broader.

Charlie leapt to his feet and let out a loud whoop. 'Negative,' he shouted, and thumped the table. He strode over to his locker and wrenched the door open. 'Here, catch,' he said, lobbing a bottle of pills in her direction.

Carrie laughed as she caught the medication. She joined him at the rubbish bin near the sink. Charlie pushed down on the pedal, the lid opened and he emptied the contents of his containers into the bin. Carrie followed suit, watching the pills flow out like a waterfall. She threw the empty bottle in after them.

'Negative,' Charlie repeated. He looked down into her sparkling eyes and felt a swell of desire surge in his chest. She was smiling, her lips glistening with the gloss she wore. Her chest rose and fell, the soft navy blouse she was wearing beneath her jacket straining at the cleavage. He wanted to touch it to see what it was made out of. Hell, he just wanted to touch her.

He picked her up and swung her round and round, ending up in the centre of the room.

'Put me down, Charlie,' Carrie protested, laughing hard and

hanging on tight to his arms. She could feel the solid muscle beneath her hands and suppressed the urge to run her hand up under his sleeve.

Charlie placed her back on the floor, laughing. 'Thank you.' His heart was hammering and he was slightly breathless from his spontaneous act.

'My pleasure,' Carrie replied, and then wished she had chosen her words more carefully as she watched his gaze grow hot like molten metal and his pupils dilate.

'No, the pleasure was all mine.' Charlie noticed a flare of flame heat her whiskey eyes and her soft lips part. His gaze settled on her lips. They were full and moist and inviting and he wanted to kiss her. Very, very much. He remembered how responsive she'd been that night at her place and needed to feel her against him again.

'Carrie,' he whispered.

She felt caught in a bubble. The world faded away and there was just the two of them. Her mouth, her lips suddenly felt as dry as the Sahara and she moistened them, her tongue flicking out to wet them.

Charlie followed the darting movement and groaned. It was all the encouragement he needed. He dropped his head and claimed her mouth. It tasted like honey and he was instantly addicted. He deepened the kiss and a shot of adrenaline buzzed through his system as his tongue stroked across her bottom lip. He wanted more. He wanted to push her back against the table and feel her legs wrap around his waist. His hand trembled as it slid beneath her jacket and smoothed the soft silk of her blouse where her waist curved into her hip.

Carrie was drowning. Suffocating. Dying. This was madness. Pure madness. They had to stop. They were at work. But his mouth felt so good and his hand was hot where it touched her and she wanted him to move it higher. To feel the heat against her breasts. Her nipples hardened instantly.

No! No! No! This was insane. Carrie wrenched her mouth away with difficulty, her chest heaving, her pulse points bounding. The look of naked desire in his gaze, the unsteadiness of his breath called to her and she took a step back out of temptation's reach.

'Carrie.' He took a step towards her.

His voice was husky and she felt a surge of heat between her legs. 'No.' She shook her head and held out her hand to ward him off.

The door opened and they both started. 'So, are the results in yet?' Joe asked, bustling into the room. 'Oh, hi, Carrie.' Joe walked between them, oblivious to the tension. 'It's OK, we can talk later,' he said, flicking on the kettle.

Charlie ran a hand through his hair, his gaze not leaving Carrie's face. 'It's OK,' he said. 'Carrie knows.'

Joe leant against the sink. 'Oh, right. So?'

Charlie broke eye contact with Carrie and looked at Joe. 'Negative.'

'Aha! That's great.' Joe surged forward and wrapped his friend in a big bear hug. He slapped him on the back. 'Woohoo! After a year of abstinence it's going to be a hot time in the old town tonight, my friend.'

Charlie looked back towards Carrie, who was now busying herself with her things.

'We're still on for The Mill tonight?'

Charlie wasn't really listening to his friend. He was too busy watching Carrie withdraw into her shell. The woman who had just kissed him into oblivion hiding behind her papers and pinstripes.

'Charlie!'

'Hmm, what? Oh…yes,' he said distractedly.

Carrie ground her teeth as she powered up her laptop and then castigated herself for her reaction. Why wouldn't he be out there again? A year was a long time for a virile male to go without, wasn't it? She thought about her own nearly five-year record and felt suddenly depressed. It hadn't seemed to matter until now.

'Charlie.' Angela bustled into the room. 'Your first patient's here.'

'Right,' he said, still staring at Carrie. He willed her to look at him but she tapped away on her keyboard instead. 'See you later, Carrie,' he said.

'Uh-uh,' Carrie replied, staring resolutely at the screen.

Carrie dragged herself into work the next morning after a sleepless night. Every time she'd shut her eyes the kiss had replayed in her head and heat had surged through her body, making sleep impossible. And then she'd got angry with herself. She'd bet Charlie wasn't lying awake, tortured by images of their kiss. He was, no doubt, making out with some babe he'd picked up, their intimate moment completely forgotten in his rush to get laid.

But it became apparent quite quickly that Charlie was as grumpy, if not grumpier, than her. Carrie raised an eyebrow at Joe as Charlie snapped at him over something trivial and stormed back to his office.

'I take it no one fancied him last night?' The idea seemed ludicrous to her but he certainly wasn't acting like a man who'd spent a night divesting himself of a year's worth of sexual frustration.

'Are you kidding? They were swarming. He just wasn't interested. If I were him, I would have been champing at the bit to clean out…' Joe stopped in mid-sentence, realising it was hardly an appropriate thing to say in front of a lady. 'Er…sorry, well, you get my gist.'

Carrie laughed. 'Yes, Joe. I get your gist.'

'I think celibacy has fried some of his brain cells.'

Carrie felt stupidly smug and surprisingly happy that

Charlie hadn't cheapened their kiss by going out and finding himself a convenient warm body the very same day. Not that the kiss had meant anything, of course. It had just been a crazy spur-of-the-moment celebratory thing. Pure reaction to good news. A release of pent-up emotions. She knew that. But still…maybe it *had* meant more to him?

By lunchtime the next day, however, Carrie was wishing Charlie had got laid. They all were. His mood seemed to get worse as each minute passed. Angela and Joe were ready to have him committed. Joe had decided not to even come to the clinic and play basketball at lunchtime and Angela, who usually ate in the staffroom, decided that anywhere but the centre would be a good place to eat her lunch.

Carrie was working through lunch as usual, munching on a sandwich at the front desk while she performed a data search on Angela's computer. Two girls came rushing in the front door.

'Help.'

Carrie looked up over the bench. One of the girls was heavily pregnant and clutching at her stomach. She didn't look any older than sixteen and was panting furiously.

'Charlie,' Carrie called, raising her voice as she rushed to the girl's aid. 'What's wrong?'

'She's having the baby.'

Charlie strode out of his office. 'Treatment room,' he urged.

'What's your name?' Carrie asked as she ushered the girls into the room.

'Donna,' the pregnant one panted, sobbing and panting at the same time.

'How pregnant are you?' Carrie asked, helping her up onto the high bed.

The girl cried out as another contraction swept through her and clutched at Carrie's shoulder.

'We don't know,' her friend said. 'She's never seen a doctor.'

Charlie saw the look of surprise on Carrie's face. It was common enough around these parts. The labouring girl looked like a street kid if her general unkempt appearance was anything to go by. Street kids rarely sought any antenatal care.

'How long have the pains been coming for?' Carrie kept going, her mind sorting methodically through the required information.

'They started about half an hour ago and they've just been getting worse.'

'Have her membranes ruptured?' Carrie asked.

Both girls looked at her blankly.

'Have your waters broken?' Charlie intervened.

Unless you worked in this area, it was hard to remember that medical terms weren't well understood in this neck of the woods. He'd been pleasantly surprised, though, at how Carrie had taken control. He could see her brain working behind her eyes. The brain of a doctor.

'No,' Donna replied.

'I'll call an ambulance,' Charlie said.

He was back in two minutes and Carrie felt the tension in her shoulders ease a little. She'd delivered babies before, but never out of the comfort zone of a hospital.

'Here,' Charlie said, pulling a pre-packaged birthing kit out of a cupboard. 'I'll open this. Why don't you do an examination?'

Carrie glanced at him. *Her?* He handed her some gloves and nodded and smiled at her. *Her.* She swallowed. She could do this. She'd done it before. Charlie certainly had faith in her.

The gloves took for ever to get on over her shaking hands. She could hear Charlie talking soothingly to Donna in the background. Carrie lifted Donna's dress and knew instantly she wouldn't need to do a vaginal examination.

'How far away is the ambulance?' she asked.

'Ten,' he said.

'We don't have ten minutes—the head's right there. It's crowned.'

Charlie could see the panic in her gaze that she was trying hard to quell. 'All righty, then,' he said calmly. 'Looks like we're going to deliver a baby.'

'But—'

'Carrie, babies that come this fast don't usually need anything from us. All you need to do is catch.'

Carrie stared into his calm grey gaze. He looked in control. Confident. She nodded.

Catch.

'OK, Donna, next contraction, big push,' Charlie said from his position at the head of the bed. 'Your baby's nearly out.'

They had only seconds to wait before Donna started moaning again.

'That's it, Donna, big push, good job,' Carrie encouraged as the girl shut her eyes and bellowed as she bore down, clenching her fists.

'Head's out,' Carrie called, caught up in the excitement and expectation of new life. 'One more push with the next contraction and it'll be all over.'

Donna pushed with all her might and the rest of the baby slipped out into Carrie's waiting hands. 'It's a girl,' she announced, grinning madly at Charlie as he handed her a sterile green towel to wrap around the already vigorously squawking, pink newborn.

Donna was crying and so was her friend. Even Carrie felt tears prick the backs of her eyes. The start of new life never ceased to awe her. She passed the baby to her mother. 'She's beautiful,' Carrie said.

'Well done, Carrie,' Charlie said, grinning at her as he came down to join her at the business end, handing her some cord clamps.

He watched Donna with her newborn, extraordinarily moved by the instinctive bonding that was taking place on front of him. The new mother's eyes were shut and she was rubbing her cheek against her little girl's forehead. The baby's tiny perfect hand was touching Donna's face. How must it feel to hold your baby for the first time?

Donna may have had no antenatal education or read a hundred books on becoming a mother, but she was forming an immediate attachment with her baby. He heard a noise behind him.

'Ambulance is here.'

Carrie turned and noticed the two officers standing in the doorway while she was still basking in Charlie's praise. At least the frown he'd been wearing for the last two days had lifted. He was the Charlie from Wednesday, from the day he'd kissed her. His eyes glowed with warmth and happiness.

A joint decision was made to deliver the placenta and then transfer Donna to hospital. 'You can do it,' Charlie said.

Carrie nodded, feeling a confidence she hadn't felt in a long time. The placenta was delivered ten minutes later and Charlie held out a plastic bag for Carrie to place it in. It had to go to the hospital with Donna so it could be checked thoroughly in case it hadn't been completely expelled.

Carrie was very conscious of Charlie as they stood side by side, watching the ambulance depart. His arm brushed against hers occasionally and it felt warm. It reminded her of the heat from his hand the other day and she felt her stomach clench involuntarily.

'What happened?' Angela asked, returning to the clinic in time to see the ambulance pull away from the kerb.

'We just delivered a baby.' Charlie smiled.

Angela looked at him incredulously and then threw back her head and laughed. 'If I'd have known a baby was going to put a smile back on your face again, Charlie Wentworth, I would have put you in a taxi and sent you to the nearest labour ward.'

Angela continued to chuckle as she brushed past them.

'What the hell did she mean by that?' he grumbled, staring after his receptionist.

Carrie pressed her lips together hard to stop herself from laughing. 'Wouldn't know.' She shrugged and also left his side.

Charlie watched Carrie's pinstriped rear disappear down the hallway. He watched Angela busying herself at the desk. *Women!*

CHAPTER SEVEN

CHARLIE pulled up outside Carrie's house and switched off his engine. The smell of Chinese takeaway permeated the car and he hesitated with his hand on the door. *Damn it all!* This didn't have to be a big deal. He was just having a meal with a colleague.

And her very cute daughter.

In her apartment.

Where he had intimate knowledge of her bedroom.

No. It was just a thank you. For today and the other day when she'd opened the envelope and because he knew he'd been unbearable the last couple of days. And it was this or let Joe drag him out to another seedy bar with women who didn't do anything for him. *Any more.*

He pushed open the car door determinedly, grabbed the plastic bag and the bottle of wine and headed towards the building. He soon arrived at her apartment and rapped on the door before he changed his mind. He only hoped they hadn't already eaten. He checked his watch. Six o'clock. Carrie opened the door.

'Oh.' Carrie blinked. *Charlie was standing at her door.* For an awful second she wondered if her over-active imagination had conjured him up. 'Charlie?'

She was dressed in tie-dyed clothes again, T-shirt and shorts.

Her hair was down. He liked it. He liked it a lot. 'I hope you haven't already eaten. I bought Dana's favourite—Chinese.'

'Oh,' she said again, her brain freezing. What did this mean? What did he want? Memories of what had happened last time they'd stood at this door swamped her.

Stop it!

'Isn't this a little early for you to be leaving the centre?'

He smiled. 'I'm getting a life.'

Carrie's breath caught at the hint of a promise lurking behind the teasing glint in his grey gaze.

'Mummy?'

'Here, darling.' Carrie turned, grateful for the interruption.

Charlie smiled at Dana as she approached. She had on a T-shirt and shorts with paint stains all over them. She even had a smudge of paint on her face. 'Hi, Sleeping Beauty.'

Dana's eyes lit up. 'Charlie!' She threw out her arms and hugged his legs.

Charlie looked down at her blonde head and felt a swell of tenderness deep inside. He felt honoured to be so easily accepted into Dana's world. And a little scared. He crouched down. 'You look like you fell into a paint can,' he teased.

'Mummy said the same thing.' Dana giggled.

Charlie looked up at Carrie. There was confusion in her eyes. He looked back at Dana. 'Hah! Great minds think alike.'

'Did you bringed your dukebox?' Dana asked, looking over Charlie's shoulder.

He laughed. 'No, but I bought something just as good.' He held up the plastic bag. 'Ding rolls.'

'Oh, look, Mummy,' Dana said. 'Charlie bought us Chinese.'

Carrie smiled and stroked her daughter's fringe. 'Yes, darling. We'd better invite him in, then.'

Carrie stood aside and motioned for Charlie to precede her. He brushed past her and she could smell his aftershave, mingled with the aroma of Chinese cooking, and it was a temptingly spicy combination.

'So you haven't eaten?' he asked as he plonked the bag and wine on the marble-topped bench.

Carrie shook her head, lifting Dana up to sit on the bench. 'Friday and Saturday nights are Susie's nights off.'

'She's my nanny,' Dana interjected proudly.

'Friday night is usually too-tired-to-cook night and we have another of Dana's favourites—two-minute noodles.' She held up the packet. She'd been just about to add hot water to it when he'd knocked.

'Yummy, two-minute noodles,' Charlie said.

'You like them, too?' Dana asked.

He nodded. He'd practically lived on them and frozen TV dinners since his separation from Veronica. He was rarely home early enough to be bothered to actually cook anything from scratch. That was what Sunday dinners with his parents were for. For him anyway. They usually had an entirely different agenda.

'It's girls' night in,' Dana told him, swinging her legs.

'Oh?' He quirked an eyebrow at Carrie.

'It's nothing,' she said dismissively. 'We eat noodles, she gets to drink watered-down orange juice out of a plastic wine-glass, I let her stay up a bit later and we put on a CD and dance.'

He shut his eyes and groaned. 'And I've just gatecrashed?' *Good one, Charlie.*

'It's OK. There'll be plenty more.'

'Will you dance with us, Charlie?' Dana asked.

He looked into her eyes and was unable to resist. 'Of course.'

'OK, let's get this food organised,' Carrie said briskly, her heart contracting at the look that passed between her daughter and the man who not even two weeks ago had ravaged her in her bedroom.

Charlie uncorked the wine while Carrie retrieved three

plates. She removed the containers from the plastic bag and took their lids off, steam sending a delicious aroma circulating around the kitchen. Dana was allowed to pour her own orange juice.

'Come on, Sleeping Beauty,' Charlie said, lifting Dana off the bench and setting her down. He picked up two plates and followed Carrie through to the dining room.

Charlie had never laughed so much in his life than he did over dinner. Dana kept them distracted from each other. She was a truly delightful child. Her smile was angelic, her voice melodic and her laughter wicked. She was captivating. Why the hell were Sunday lunches never this much fun with his family?

They were so stiff and formal. Everyone dressed up, definitely no paint stains or tie-dye. His siblings and their assorted partners tried to outdo each other with their latest published paper or research grant. The menu was cordon bleu—no two-minute anything allowed. And his father pontificated and preached and tried to convert him to one specialty or another. He dreaded them. In fact, he only really attended them out of a mixture of duty and guilt.

But this? This evening with Carrie and her daughter showed him the way a real family conducted itself. With warmth and laughter and sharing. He'd never had such a sense of family as he'd had tonight. He doubted he ever had. From as early as he could remember, things had been stiff and formal and the pressure to perform had been there. This relaxed, laughter-filled meal was like a breath of fresh air. He desperately wanted in on this scene of domestic bliss, but a part of him held back. Upbringing was a hard act to beat, and his childhood had been the complete opposite of Dana's. What if he got involved and then messed it up?

He felt a pang in his chest as he watched Carrie wipe Dana's mouth, and couldn't decide if it was envy or lust. He suspected from the tightness in his loins it was the latter, but there was no denying he coveted what Carrie and Dana had.

'Come on, you, bathtime,' Carrie said. She could feel Charlie's gaze on her and if she didn't move now she might just do something ridiculous, like lean into him and rub her cheek against his chest. The situation was hopelessly intimate, all of them sitting here, laughing and chatting like a family. It was hard not to weave fantasies.

'I want Charlie to do it,' Dana said.

Oh, no. No. No. No. That would be too much like happy families. 'No, sweetie. Charlie's going to do the dishes. Aren't you?' She turned to him and raised an eyebrow.

He could see the gentle note of warning in her eyes. 'Absolutely.' He nodded. 'I love washing up.'

Carrie shot him a small smile.

'You are going to stay for the dancing, aren't you, Charlie?' Dana looked up at him, pleading with her big blue eyes.

Charlie saw Carrie roll her eyes and smothered a smirk. 'Wild horses couldn't keep me away,' he promised. 'Now, go have your bath.'

Dana turned to do his bidding obediently and Carrie rolled her eyes at Charlie again. His warm sexy chuckle followed her all the way to the bathroom.

Fifteen minutes later the dishes were done and Dana was padding down the hallway, her wet hair combed, her thumb in her mouth, dragging her blanky behind her. She had on some tie-dyed pyjamas.

'Do you like my pyjamas, Charlie?' Dana asked, pirouetting.

He looked up as Carrie entered behind Dana. 'Very much,' he said.

'My aunty makes them. She's a niner.'

'Oh?' he said, shooting a puzzled look at Carrie.

'A designer,' Carrie clarified.

'A niner.' Dana nodded. 'She loves tie-tie the best.'

'Tie-dye,' Carrie corrected.

'Ah.' He nodded sagely.

Dana walked towards him and stopped in front of him. She put her head all the way back to peer up at him. 'Come on, Charlie, Mummy, it's dance time.' Dana slipped her hand into Charlie's and tugged.

He laughed and followed.

'We don't have a dukebox, do we, Mummy?' Dana asked, not bothering to wait for a reply before she ploughed on. 'We have a DD player.'

'Ah.' Charlie nodded. 'A DD player. Cool.'

'Can we have "Crocodile Rock", Mummy?'

Carrie smiled. 'Sure sweetie.'

Carrie put the Elton John CD in the player and fast forwarded to Dana's current favourite. She could feel Charlie's stare and her hand shook as she pressed the play button.

'Come on, Charlie,' Dana said pulling him up from the lounge. 'Dance with me.'

Carrie sat back and laughed and smiled and clapped as her daughter twisted and bopped energetically with a grinning Charlie. She looked so happy it was almost painful. This was what it could have been like if Rupert had stuck around. Well, actually, she couldn't quite imagine stiff-lipped Rupert letting his hair down this much, but didn't every little girl have a right to a father?

Dana was looking at Charlie as if he was the best thing since sliced bread. She already talked about him non-stop as it was. It was easy to see that she could become very attached to Charlie. God knew, she was having enough trouble forgetting him.

But in another week or so she'd be finished at the centre and she'd never see Charlie again. And as much fun as this moment was, as wonderful as it was to see Dana so happy, she had to make sure Charlie didn't come around again. For both their sakes. They'd already overstepped the line a couple of times and it was imperative she keep it professional. Charlie was a flash in the pan as far as her life goals went, and it would be foolish to allow him to distract her from what was important.

The song began for the fourth time and Carrie rose off the lounge to turn it off. It was already seven-thirty—way past Dana's bedtime.

'I think that's more than enough, young lady.'

'No, Mummy,' Dana pleaded. 'You haven't danced with me yet. Can we dance like we always do before I go to bed?'

Dana's blue-eyed stare and earnest face could have won her an Oscar. 'OK…but just once.'

Dana jumped up and down and Carrie put on 'Endless Love.' She picked up a waiting Dana, who snuggled into her side and stuck her thumb in her mouth. 'Blanky,' she murmured, looking around for the tatty piece of polar fleece she'd had since a baby.

'Here.' Charlie pulled it out from under where he was sitting on the lounge.

Carrie tried to tune Charlie out as she slowly swayed around the lounge room with Dana. Their girls' night in always ended with 'Endless Love'. It was one of her favourite rituals of the week with Dana snuggled close and the soaring romantic music swirling all around them. It seemed strange to have a third party sharing this mother-daughter moment. Unfortunately it didn't feel bad strange. It felt…nice strange. Cosy.

Dana roused. 'Charlie.' She held out her hand to him.

Charlie looked at Carrie and their gazes held. He desperately wanted to go. To take Dana's hand and envelop them both in his arms and pull them close. But he knew there was a line he'd be crossing. One he wasn't entirely sure Carrie wanted him to cross. Wasn't entirely sure he was ready to cross himself.

Carrie saw the yearning in his eyes and knew she didn't have the heart to deny him entry into their circle. Neither did she want to. She had actually felt tonight what it would be like to have a man in her life, someone for her and Dana, and she didn't have the power as the song swirled around her to end it all. She would have to, she knew. But surely they could just have the song?

Charlie saw the barely perceptible nod of her head and he rose from the chair. The lure of mother and daughter was too powerful to resist. His heart thudded as he took Dana's hand and let her pull him closer. He swayed in unison with them, trying to keep a little distance. His gaze locked with Carrie's and he saw desire heat her eyes and dilate her pupils.

'Closer, Charlie,' a drowsy Dana demanded, pulling him in more.

Charlie swallowed as his body moved closer to Carrie's, their gazes still locked. It seemed like the most natural thing in the world to put his arm around Dana's waist. And Carrie's. Draw them in close. Tuck Carrie's head in beneath his chin. She didn't resist. His heart beat loudly. Was hers?

Carrie resisted the urge to rub her cheek against his shirt for about ten seconds. But his scent, his warmth, the sheer bulk of him pressed against her cheek made it impossible to ignore. She turned her face into his chest and rubbed her nose against the fabric of his shirt. It smelt like soap, sweet and sour pork and man.

There was nothing but the three of them and the music. Even Dana, who was practically asleep, was forgotten in the cloud of lust and longing that enveloped her. Charlie was making her think of parts of her body that she hadn't thought about in a long time. Heating places, igniting places, stroking places that she'd forgotten she had.

The song came to an end, they stopped swaying and for a brief moment they didn't move. She could hear his heart thudding loudly against her ear and wondered if he could also hear hers.

'Mummy?' Dana stirred.

Carrie blinked. It took a second to remember where the hell she was. She pulled her head off Charlie's chest and took a step away from him. 'Hush, sweetie, you fell asleep. Off to bed with you.' She dropped a kiss on her daughter's head.

''Night, Charlie,' Dana murmured, fluttering her eyelashes half-open.

''Night, Sleeping Beauty,' Charlie crooned, leaning forward slightly to also drop a kiss on her head. He looked at Carrie as he withdrew, her lips so very, very close. So full and soft. So inviting. The heat in her eyes flared again and it took all his willpower to pull away.

Carrie walked on very unsteady legs to Dana's bedroom and tucked her daughter in. She stroked her fringe, staring down at her rosy cheeks, her mouth slack around her inserted thumb. Lying before her was her whole world. For just over four years nothing else but Dana had mattered. She had taken up Carrie's whole emotional existence.

But outside in her lounge room was a man who was slowly pushing his way into her heart, too. Did she have room? And, as good as he was with Dana, would he have room in his heart for her daughter? The night he had run out when confronted with the reality of Dana was still fresh in her mind. They came as a package deal and she didn't have the time or emotional strength to deal with another man who didn't want them both.

She snapped on Dana's bedside light and lingered for one last look at her beautiful girl. She looked so pure, so innocent. Carrie knew she couldn't risk that on a man who was probably just looking for someone to break the drought with.

She straightened. He had to go. She doubted she'd be strong enough to resist him if he stayed any longer. All she had to do was turn around, march into the lounge room, thank him for the meal and show him the door. She could do that. She *could* do that.

Charlie felt as if time and reality had slowed right down. He felt as if his blood flowed sluggishly through his veins, his heart banged painfully at a snail's pace, his breath shortened dramatically until he was light-headed from lack of oxygen. And he ached everywhere. His arms ached. His chest ached. His groin ached.

Carrie entered the room and she was talking about the meal and thanking him but nothing other than the bound of his blood and *Kiss her* could be heard through the goulash-type soup his brain had become. He stood as she approached.

'And I really think it would be best if you—'

His kiss cut her off. His hands cradled her face as his hot lips ravished hers. His impatient tongue demanded entry into her mouth. She tasted like red wine and honey chicken and he couldn't get enough of it. Of her. He heard her moan, felt her clutch at his shirt, heard her ragged breath.

He released her mouth but kept her body pressed against his. 'I want you.'

Carrie could see the haze of lust in his grey gaze and, God help her, she wanted him, too. Wanted his shirt off so she could inhale the scent of his naked skin. Wanted all his clothes off. She wanted to smell him everywhere. Touch him everywhere. Kiss him everywhere. He was looking at her like he wanted to devour her and her internal muscles clenched at the almost savage desire she saw there. She didn't have the willpower to turn him away.

But a tiny speck of good sense prevailed. 'You have to be gone by morning,' she croaked.

He thought about it for one second. 'Done,' he said, lowering his head swiftly to reclaim her mouth.

Carrie grabbed his shirt at the back and pulled it up. His skin. She had to touch his skin. He angled his head so she could yank it off, breaking their kiss. She pushed her face greedily against his chest. His skin was warm and it felt solid and smelt divine as she dropped kisses along the flat plane of his pectoral muscle.

Charlie dragged a breath in as her tongue darted out and moistened his nipple. He felt his groin respond immediately. 'Enough,' he growled, pulling away. He grasped the hem of her shirt and pulled it over her head in record time.

Carrie stared at the look of pure desire in his eyes as his gaze feasted on lace-covered breasts. 'Bedroom,' she demanded, knowing it would probably be her last coherent thought for the night.

Charlie didn't have to be asked twice. He swung her up into his arms and strode with her through the apartment. About the only thing his lust-drugged brain remembered was the way to her bedroom.

Charlie kissed her as he lowered her feet to the floor, his hands burying themselves in her wavy auburn locks. He heard her moan and could feel her arms clinging around his neck and he wanted to take her on the spot. But he wanted to take his time also. To look at her. To touch her. To lick her all over.

His hands stroked down her near-naked back as his kiss deepened. Her skin was soft and warm and he took his time exploring every inch. He caressed the curve of her waist, his thumb running up and down the concave smoothness. He lingered in the hollow of her back, teasing the flesh, his fingers flirting with the waistband of her shorts. She moaned against his mouth and he could sense her barely restrained control in the huskiness of her breath and the tremble of her fingers as they splayed through his hair.

Charlie was holding her so close he could feel the squash of her breasts hot against him, the lace of her bra scraping against his chest. He lifted his head. He wanted to look at her. Touch her.

Carrie whimpered as he pulled away. His mouth was like

a drug, a really addictive, really incredible drug and he'd just withdrawn her supply.

'Shh,' he hushed her, running a finger over her lips. 'I want to look at you.'

Carrie blushed and was grateful that the only light in the room was from the streetlight outside. The way his gaze devoured her breasts was doing funny things to her breathing and she felt weak at the knees, knowing he wanted her that much.

And then his finger ran along the edge of the lace and her nipples hardened instantly and everything heated inside. It was incredibly erotic, watching his fingers stroke over the lace, and she felt herself sway, her eyes closing on a swell of longing. And then his lips were stroking heat up her neck and behind her ear, his fingers toying with her bra clasp.

Charlie struggled uselessly with the clasp, his fingers clumsy in his rush to touch her. No matter how hard he tried he didn't seem to be able to unhook the bra.

Carrie was so involved with the fire he was igniting along her collar-bone she didn't even register his trouble.

'I'm sorry,' he said. 'I guess I'm out of practice. It's been a while.'

It took a second for Carrie to figure out what he was talking about. 'Oh.' She grinned. 'I bet it hasn't been as long as me.'

He smiled back, stroking a stray lock of her hair out of her eyes. 'Maybe not. But a year's a long time.'

'Huh,' she said dismissively. 'Try nearly five.'

Charlie chuckled. 'No, thanks.' He sobered. 'It's OK, it's one of those things you never forget.'

She was captivated by his intense gaze. 'Are you sure?' she whispered.

He nodded slowly. 'Now, if you wouldn't mind taking this off…' he ran an index finger around a lace-covered nipple '…I'll demonstrate.'

Carrie's hands shook as she reached behind and unclasped

her bra. She could barely breathe from the blaze in his eyes. She removed it slowly, suddenly shy. No one but Dana had seen her naked in four years. The urge to cover herself was strong and she raised her hands to cross them across her chest.

'No,' he whispered, exerting gentle pressure on her arms, and was gratified when they fell by her sides. He felt his loins stir as he took in the beauty of her breasts. Her nipples were scrunched hard in the centre of all her lush fullness. 'I've been fantasising what lay beneath those damn buttons for weeks.'

His voice was husky and she again felt herself sway towards him. When he reached out and cupped them, ran a thumb over each nipple, she gasped out loud. 'Please,' she whispered. She had no idea what she'd said it for but when he swept her close, lowered his head and covered one rosy peak with his mouth, she knew exactly why.

'Oh!'

He pushed her back against the bed and then it was just a swirl of sensation. The heaviness of his body pinning her to the bed. The hardness of his erection as his maleness encompassed her. The thrill of his touch against her skin. The pleasure of his tongue at her pulse points. The eroticism of his bite as he used his teeth as a weapon of sweet, sensual torture.

She wasn't sure where her gasps ended and his groans began. Whose pounding heart reverberated through her body? His or hers? Whose irregular breathing echoed in her ears? His or hers? They seemed to have morphed into one being. One entity. Locked in a mating frenzy. A sexual bubble. Not knowing or caring where one began and the other one finished.

Charlie's hand slipped beneath her waistband, beneath the lacy elastic of her knickers. Carrie groaned out loud and bit into his shoulder as his fingers sought and found her centre. They felt so good inside her she thought she was going to reach orgasm just from their pressure alone.

She reached down and undid his fly, pushed his underwear

aside, filled her hands with his proud, surging manhood. She heard his sharp indrawn breath and stroked her finger around the tip.

'Carrie,' he groaned.

She smiled against his mouth. 'What?' she asked, grasping him and stroking her hand up and down.

'Carrie,' Charlie growled. He wasn't sure how long he'd be able to hold out if she kept that up. He held his hand firmly against hers. 'Later. Right now I think you need to get out of those clothes.'

He pushed himself away from her, snagging his hand in her waistband and dragging her shorts and knickers over her hips and down her legs in one swoop. He grinned down at her. She was completely naked now.

'You, too.' She raised a leg and placed her foot against his hardness, feeling him twitch. 'Take 'em off.'

Charlie laughed, divested himself of the remainder of his clothes and climbed back on the bed, hovering above her on his hands and knees. He watched her raise her head off the bed, her lips seeking his. He dipped his head, letting her claim his mouth, probe it with her tongue.

He pulled away and grinned at her moan of protest. He grinned even more at her 'yes' as he lowered his mouth to first one nipple then the other. He revelled in her low moan as he licked down to her belly button, ran wet circles around it and delved inside. And he exulted in her 'Charlie!' as he moved lower and found her sweet hot centre.

Carrie almost combusted at the touch of his tongue against her. He found the right spot instantly and she felt her hips rise off the bed involuntarily. His tongue flicked expertly and she could hear her cries of pleasure on an abstract level only. And when he pushed a finger inside and then pulled it out before plunging in again, mimicking the ultimate sexual act, she cried out louder because she was shattering into pieces and nothing could hold the shuddering of her body in check.

Charlie covered her mouth with his as his finger continued to stroke, stoke, sate. Swallowing her primal cries was dizzying, satisfying beyond his wildest dreams. He had made her come apart. He had made her pulse around his finger. He had made her crazy with lust. She devoured his mouth and he plundered hers in return, sucking up every last moan and whimper as her orgasm subsided.

'Charlie.' A depleted Carrie floated back down to earth.

He laughed and kissed her again hard, gathering her close, rolling over so she lay on top of him. His hands pressed against her buttocks, pressing her into the jut of his still rock-hard erection.

Carrie roused herself. She kissed his mouth, his eyes, his shoulder. 'Let's do that again.'

He chuckled. 'I'm ready.'

'Yes, indeed you are.' She smiled, rubbing herself against the hard ridge of his sex.

'Carrie,' he warned.

She kissed him hard on the mouth. 'Please, tell me you have condoms.'

'Wallet. Back pocket.' Joe had given them to him on Wednesday night.

Carrie grinned, leaping off the bed, locating his discarded clothes and finding a foil packet. She held it up triumphantly and ripped it open with her teeth. Within seconds she had Charlie covered and he had pulled her down on the bed, trapping her beneath him, biting her neck as he slowly entered her.

'Oh, yes,' he groaned as her tightness surrounded him.

'Again,' she whispered into his ear, the one stroke nowhere near enough.

Charlie obliged.

'Oh, yes,' Carrie breathed into his ear.

And obliged again.

'More,' she whispered.

And again.

'Oh, God, don't stop,' she whimpered.

Stop? Was she mad? 'Carrie,' he cried as the pressure in his loins built to unbearable proportions.

She felt so good around him, underneath him. He wanted to pound inside her for ever, hold close like this for ever, be joined with her like this for ever. But the pressure was working against him, taking over, beyond his control, and he cried out her name as it erupted, pulsing like a molten lava flow through his veins, buzzing like an electric current through every cell in his body. And finally spilling out to cover his body in white-hot ecstasy.

Carrie cried out, too, as her body became embroiled in the heat and rush of her own orgasm. It was even more powerful than the last. Her body was buffeted by shock waves more violent than the last. Like the waves emanating from a nuclear explosion. An internal mushroom cloud rippling through all the cells of her body. And all she could do was hold onto Charlie, anchor herself to him as they wreaked their erotic havoc.

The tumult rose to a crescendo and then slowly, slowly Charlie came down from the heights. Carrie was still spasming around him and the odd shudder quaked through his muscles. They were silent, like feathers floating to the ground, only their heavy breathing breaking the quiet.

'See,' Charlie murmured a few moments later, kissing her hair, 'I told you. Not bad for an out-of-practice couple.'

CHAPTER EIGHT

CHARLIE woke the next morning, sun streaming in through the window, a little finger lifting his eyelid.

'You had a sleepover, Charlie?'

Oh, hell! Charlie opened both eyes. Dana's smiling face greeted him. He felt Carrie, who was snuggled into his back, stiffen. 'Morning, Sleeping Beauty.'

Oh, damn, damn, damn. 'Darling,' Carrie said, rising up on her elbow to look over Charlie's shoulder, amazed at how much she wanted to bite it, even confronted with a truly horrible situation.

'I'm hungry,' Dana said. 'Do you know how to make pancakes, Charlie?'

'Ah…yes, I do, actually,' he said, despite Carrie's finger poking into his ribs.

'Come on, then. Pancakes are Mummy's favourite.' Dana pulled at the edge of the sheet.

'Darling!' Carrie said, grabbing the sheet and holding it fast to Charlie's flat stomach. 'Why don't you go and get the bowl and jug and eggs out and Charlie will join you in just a moment?'

'OK,' Dana said agreeably. She dropped the sheet and skipped out, dragging blanky behind her.

Carrie collapsed back, groaning, and stared at the ceiling. Charlie pressed his lips together really hard to stop himself from laughing. He knew this was bad. Very bad. That Dana could read things into this that he wasn't sure he was capable of, but after an amazing night he was relaxed enough to see the humour in the situation.

Carrie punched him lightly on the arm. 'This is not funny, Charlie.'

He chuckled out loud as he stared into her mortified face.

'You were supposed to be gone two hours ago!'

'I know, I know, but you wanted to snuggle for just a bit longer and, well, frankly, you wore me out. I just closed my eyes for a second.'

'This is a disaster,' Carrie muttered, trying not to think about the eyeful her daughter would have had if she'd managed to pull back that sheet. Or how they'd made love over and over until the wee small hours. Even when their supply of four condoms had run out, Charlie had laid her back and made it all about her.

Charlie should have been concerned. He should have been worried, too, but he was too happy at this moment to care. He hadn't felt this good since before his marriage had fallen apart. He rose from the bed and stretched languorously.

Carrie swallowed hard as she watched his naked buttocks tighten and his muscles undulate through his broad tanned back. *Oh, God, the things he had done to her.* 'Charlie, for heaven's sake, put something on. Dana could wander in here any second.'

Charlie turned and grinned down at her. He saw her gaze widen as she stared at his naked body. He felt himself twitch at the desire he saw in her eyes. 'Are you sure?' He smiled.

His voice was deep and lazy and sexy and she wanted to reach out to him and pull him back into bed. 'Charlie,' she warned.

He laughed and hunted down his clothes. 'My shirt is in the lounge room.'

Carrie groaned again. 'Great.'

He looked at her lying in bed, the sheet pulled primly up to her chin. He suppressed the urge to yank the sheet down and just stare at her. She couldn't hide behind her morning-after primness with him. Not when he knew every delicious inch of her body.

'Are you getting up or shall Dana and I make you breakfast in bed?'

Dana and I. The way he'd said it had been so possessive it scared the hell out of her. It was something a father would do with his daughter. A partner would do. But he wasn't Dana's father and he wasn't *her* partner. To get caught up in this little fantasy was dangerous. 'No. I'll have a quick shower and be out in a flash.'

'Sounds like fun.' He grinned.

Carrie felt her toes curl at the flirtatious tone and promise in his grey eyes. This was insane. *Do not read anything into this!* 'Go, Charlie, now.'

He chuckled. 'OK, OK, I'm going.'

Charlie scanned the lounge room for his missing shirt. He was looking under the lounge when Dana found him.

'Here's your shirt, Charlie,' she said, holding it out. 'Did it get hot last night?'

Oh, baby. It got very, very hot. 'A little,' he said, ruffling her hair and putting on his shirt. 'OK, let's make pancakes.'

Charlie laughed and joked with Dana as he cooked. She cracked him up with her four-year-old observations and her baby jokes. The longer he spent in her company the more charmed he was by her mix of exuberance and innocence. The enormity of what they'd done last night, and its implications, hit him square between the eyes as he flipped pancakes.

This little girl was looking at him as if he were God, Santa Claus and the Easter Bunny all rolled into one. He liked kids, had wanted his own. It had been the deal-breaker in his marriage. But this was reality. What did he know about four year-old girls? How could he be a good father when he'd had such a lousy example? Did he have the right to impose his in-experienced parenting on this close-knit, loving mother-and-daughter team?

'Mmm, something smells good.'

Charlie started as Carrie entered the room. He felt a warmth spread through his chest at the sound of her voice and he smiled at her gently, despite his chaotic thoughts. Her hair was damp from the shower and he wanted her all over again. He cursed his weak body.

'Charlie put banana in some, Mummy. They taste 'licious.'

'Hey, I tried to put banana in a few times and you wouldn't eat them,' Carrie protested, kissing Dana's head and pulling up a stool opposite Charlie at the breakfast bar.

Dana nodded solemnly. 'I know, but Charlie says you got to try everything once else how do you know whether you like it or not?'

'Does he, now?' Carrie commented. *So Charlie was the expert now, was he?*

Charlie saw the frown knit her eyebrows together. 'OK, here you go,' he said, interrupting Dana before she got him into any more trouble. He served her up two pancakes, drizzled maple syrup over them and dusted them with icing sugar. 'Eat up,' he instructed, and just because he wanted to see the frown disappear he threw in a teasing 'You need to replace those burnt calories.'

Carrie bugged her eyes at him in warning as she took the plate.

'What's calories?' Dana asked, her mouth full of pancake.

Charlie stifled a laugh at the murderous look in Carrie's eyes.

'It's how we measure energy in food,' Carrie supplied. 'Don't eat with your mouth full, sweetie.'

Charlie helped himself to seconds—he'd burnt a few calories himself last night—and wisely kept quiet. He munched away silently while Dana kept up conversation with her mother.

I could get used to this. The realisation sank in insidiously. It was domestic and homey and reeked of commitment. Everything he'd been determined to avoid. His heartbeat kicked up a notch as alarm bells started to ring. He shifted in his seat and glanced at his watch. He had to get out of there—the atmosphere was affecting his ability to think clearly. Staying last night had been a mistake.

Dana swallowed the last of her pancake. 'Can you stay all day?' she asked Charlie.

'No, darling,' Carrie interrupted before Charlie could say anything. 'Charlie has to go to work, don't you?' She sipped at her coffee, watching him furtively.

He nodded. 'Yes, I do.'

Carrie noted how quickly he agreed with her and how he'd glanced at his watch twice now in a short time. He looked ill at ease suddenly and she wondered if he was already regretting last night now the cold light of morning had thrown her life into stark reality. It shouldn't have hurt. But it did.

'Can he bring ding rolls tonight?'

'No, spring rolls aren't healthy every night. Go wash your hands, sweetie. Aren't the Wiggles on soon?'

Dana's face lit up. 'Wiggles!'

Carrie helped her off her stool and they both watched her run away to the bathroom.

Charlie smiled. 'She's a great kid.'

Carrie felt her heart contract. She could fall for him so easily. 'Yes, she is.' She started clearing the breakfast dishes. Out of the corner of her eye she saw him check his watch again. 'You'd better get going. The kids at the centre will be wondering what's happened to you.'

Charlie knew it was for the best. Knew she was giving him an out. Which was what he wanted. Wasn't it? But memories of last night still heated his loins and the experience of cooking with Dana left a lingering sense of possibility.

'Are you dismissing me, Carrie?'

Carrie scraped the plates, her back to him. 'You've looked at your watch three times in as many minutes, Charlie. You don't have to hang around. I'm a big girl. I know the score. Last night was just a very pleasant way to end a year of abstinence.' She slotted a plate into the dishwasher rack.

It sounded so callous when she said it like that. Whatever it had been, it had been more than that. 'What if it's more?'

Carrie felt her heart leap stupidly and quashed it ruthlessly as she thrust another plate into the rack. 'Right.' She forced out a trite laugh as she turned to look at him. 'More than what, Charlie? Look, let's be real for a minute. Last night was great but it wasn't real. This morning was real. A little person whose needs come before mine. I know that you get on well with Dana but I saw how quickly you bolted out of my house that first time when the reality of her existence banged you on the head. And right now you look like an animal caught in headlights.' She turned back to the dishwasher and slotted in another plate. 'You may be prepared to tolerate Dana, sweet-talk her to get in with me, but we're a team. A two-for-one deal.'

Carrie slotted in the last plate and slammed the dishwasher drawer shut.

Charlie sat very still on the stool, realising the error he'd made that night in not correcting her assumption. She still thought he'd run because of Dana's toy bringing him to his senses. And it was his fault. He'd let her think that because it had been an easy out. But it was coming back to bite him on the butt well and truly. To complicate what should have been a glorious morning after. Whatever else happened today, he had to correct this misinformation.

'No.' He stood and moved until he was standing in front of her. 'No, that's simply not true. I ran that night because I came so close to doing the one thing I swore to myself I wouldn't. I made myself a deal after the needle-stick injury— no sex. With anyone. I even threw out all my condoms and didn't buy any more in case I was ever truly tempted. And I'd made it almost to the end and then you came along. And I was so close that night and if it hadn't stopped where it did, I would have made love to you unprotected. A stupid thing to do at the best of times but with my potential to pass on a deadly disease?

'I was shocked and angry at myself that I'd put you at risk. That I'd lost control.' He stroked her cheek. 'You assumed it was because of Dana and I let you believe that because it was easier than having to explain everything. But if you believe nothing else today, please, believe this—it had absolutely nothing to do with Dana.'

Carrie saw the honesty, the sincerity in his eyes. She believed him. 'And this morning?'

He hesitated. 'She's wonderful. I adore her…'

'But.'

'I don't know anything about being a father. About four-year-old girls. I'd probably just turn out like my old man and I wouldn't wish that on any child. I don't ever want to see that wonderful light in her eyes when she looks at me go out. I don't want to start something I'd probably just screw up.'

Carrie swallowed a sudden lump of emotion and nodded. They'd both been burned by others. Still, it was good she was finding this out now before things had got too out of hand. Before her stupid heart had built castles in the air.

She wasn't used to thinking such fanciful thoughts. Rupert had hurt her really badly and she'd shut that side of her down to concentrate on Dana and her career. She'd never even thought of the possibility that another man—that love—might come around for her again.

She nodded. 'It wouldn't work.'

'Maybe if there wasn't Dana. If it was just you and me and we started a family from scratch and I could learn about being a good father from the beginning. But I don't want to ruin the beautiful dynamic that exists between you. I don't want to be responsible for that.'

'But there is Dana.' Carrie backed away, the cold metal of the sink stopping her retreat.

Charlie nodded. 'And the world is a richer place.'

She felt humbled by his words and absurdly like crying. She turned away so he couldn't see the tears shining in her eyes and leant heavily against the sink. She blinked rapidly as she gazed out the window.

Charlie's BMW sat in her driveway. It was the first time she'd seen it. Rupert had driven a Beamer. *Another rich guy?* What the hell had she been thinking?

'Dana or no Dana, I doubt it have worked anyway,' she mused.

Charlie raised an eyebrow. 'Oh?'

'We come from different backgrounds, Charlie.' She turned back to face him, feeling stronger now that this horrible awkward morning-after couldn't be laid squarely at her feet.

'Your family is practically medical royalty. My father's a taxi driver. My mother is a housewife. I have a sister who's a hairdresser and has a market stall on the weekend where she sells her tie-dye designs. I have one brother who's a mechanic and another who's a plumber. I'm the only one who went to university and that was on a scholarship. I'm very definitely a girl from the wrong side of the tracks.'

Charlie could feel a flicker of anger building in his gut. 'You think I care about any of that?'

'You will, sooner or later.' Carrie sighed. 'Your grandfather was knighted by the Queen, for God's sake. There's a building with your surname on it, Charlie.'

'Sure. And my grandfather is a snob, my father's a cold, tyrannical bore, my mother was never around and my siblings are all egocentric, self-obsessed twits. I see you with Dana and I see how childhood and families are supposed to be. I would have traded our upbringings in an instant.'

Carrie snorted. 'Well, that's easy to say when you're holding the proverbial silver spoon. When you were sheltered from the real world.'

Charlie ran an exasperated hand through his hair. 'Have you seen where I work? My clientele is largely drug addicts, hookers and homeless kids. There's nothing more real than that. Have you seen the car I drive?'

'Would that be the BMW in my driveway?'

Charlie cursed under his breath. He'd not thought about how uncomfortable a flashy status symbol would make her. 'The Datsun wouldn't start,' he said, running a frustrated hand through his hair.

'Look, Charlie, Rupert tore a hole in my heart. I was OK to sleep with for two years, but not to marry. Even carrying his child, I still wasn't good enough for his education, his six-figure bank account or his grand career plans. He hotfooted it to England and eloped with a Nobel Prize winning geneticist two months after my revelation.

'He never took me home to his parents. And the one time he visited my family he was barely civil. Now that's my fault too for being so blind, so in love, but I'm not naïve any more. I've already been rejected by one wealthy man. I don't want to set myself up for that again.'

Charlie took two paces closer. He placed a finger across her lips. 'Carrie,' he said, 'Rupert was an idiot. Please, tell me you understand that this isn't about your background. Who you are, where you're from means nothing to me. Don't lump me in with snobs like Rupert and my father.'

He looked so earnest, his thumb rubbing erotically along her bottom lip, her head was spinning. She knew he was right. There was a clarity and an honesty in his steady grey gaze that couldn't be ignored. And she'd seen enough of him in the last two weeks to know he was nothing like her ex.

He'd knelt on the road to help a stranger, he'd been gentle with a rape victim and helped an overdosed addict without batting an eyelid. He tolerated rap music, knew the complexities of street lingo and spent his lunch-hours with a group of needy boys looking for a role model. He was as far removed from Rupert as a prince from a pauper.

She nodded. 'You're right. I'm sorry. I've just been badly burned, Charlie. I had a touch of *déjà vu*.'

She leant against his chest for a brief moment, dragging herself away from him with difficulty. No matter how good it felt to be held by him, it wasn't where she belonged. She belonged with Dana. There was no place for a man who didn't want them both.

'You'd better go,' she said.

Charlie clenched and unclenched his hands. Her voice was husky and he wanted to throw caution to the wind and stay for ever. 'So where do we go from here?'

Carrie shrugged. 'Pretend it didn't happen.'

He snorted. 'Good luck with that.'

She gave him a wry smile. He was right. Last night was going to be with her for ever. 'OK, then…you're right. How about we just be adult about it? We had a great night but it's not in our destinies to go any further. Let's just shake on it and be friends.' She held out her hand.

She was right, of course. *But friends?* He nodded, took her hand and yanked her against him hard, giving her a decidedly not-friendly kiss hard on her mouth. 'Friends,' he agreed, using all his willpower to break away. 'I'll see you Monday.'

Monday morning came around and Carrie approached the front door of the clinic nervously. She'd deliberately come in later than usual, ridiculously shy at the thought of seeing

Charlie again after their intimacies. She blushed, thinking about them as she pushed through the front door.

'Morning, Angela,' she called as she passed the front desk.

The receptionist grunted at her. Carrie was still in her bad books. As far as Angela was concerned, Carrie was a threat to the centre, to her livelihood and to Charlie's. And Angela was fiercely loyal towards Charlie. She was like a pit bull guarding her territory and her master.

'Morning, Charlie,' she called, not even daring to flick a glance into his office. 'Oh!'

In one quick manoeuvre Charlie, who had leapt from his desk the moment he'd heard Carrie's voice, had grabbed her arm and yanked her into his room, kicking the door shut and pushing her roughly against it. He gave her a hungry kiss, his hands pulling the prim clasp out of her hair and luxuriating in the glide of it across his fingers.

'God, I missed you,' he muttered, his lips trekking down the line of her neck.

'Charlie,' she groaned, knowing this was highly inappropriate but stretching her neck to one side anyway to give him full access. 'I thought we'd agreed not to do this.'

'I know,' he said, plundering her lips again. 'We're not. I've just been thinking about you since yesterday. About kissing you since yesterday.' And he kissed her again.

There was a loud rap on the door. 'Police, Charlie,' Angela called.

They froze. Carrie recovered first giggling at the absurdity of the situation. She felt like a teenager who'd been caught necking by her mother.

Charlie laughed, too, as he buried his face in her neck. She smelt so good right there. So sweet. His hot breath stirred and intensified the perfume at the pulse that beat rapidly just beneath his lips. He brushed his mouth across it lightly and pushed himself away.

'Send them in,' he called, his eyes devouring the thoroughly kissed look on her face.

Carrie felt paralysed by the look of pure craving in his eyes.

'Better straighten up.' He grinned. 'You look like you've just been ravaged.'

She nodded, still not able to move.

He chuckled and reached out to straighten her collar, pull her jacket into place and hand her her clasp. He removed a trace of smeared lipstick from her mouth with his finger. Her eyes flared as he pushed the digit into her mouth and he felt a kick in his groin as she sucked it clean. He swayed towards her.

A knock sounded at the door again. Carrie gathered herself at last. 'Yes, well…' She cleared her throat, turning her back to him and pulling open the door. 'I'll get right on that, Dr Wentworth.' She smiled at the two police officers who were standing in Charlie's doorway as she departed. Carrie felt Angela's narrow-eyed stare as she slunk down the hallway.

As the week progressed their 'just friends' pact was continually breached. On Tuesday it was Joe who caught them. He'd come in the back door via the basketball court to find them in an intimate clinch in the staffroom doorway.

He slammed the door loudly and they both jumped. 'Well, well, well. Lookee here.' Joe grinned. He shook his head. 'Pinstripes. Should have guessed.'

'Hi, Joe,' Carrie said, straightening her shirt. 'This isn't what it looks like.'

Joe laughed. 'Oh? Trying to remove an obstruction from his airway with your tongue?'

Charlie laughed, too. Carrie turned and pushed his chest. 'You are not helping.'

'Next time get a room.' Joe was still grinning.

'There won't be a next time,' she said primly. 'We're just friends. Aren't we, Charlie?'

'Right…friends.'

Joe shrugged. 'OK. Whatever.'

On Thursday morning Charlie's office was empty as she passed and she popped in to look for some paperwork in his filing cabinet. He found her there a few minutes later and trapped her against it.

'Charlie, we really have to stop this,' she said as she came up for air. She was going to explode from sexual frustration if they kept this up.

He smiled and nuzzled her neck. His hand worked its way under her jacket at the back. 'I agree. This is bad…very bad.' His fingers moved round and found a lace-covered breast and he stroked it.

Carrie shut her eyes against a surge of desire. 'Charlie!'

He laughed and cut off her husky protest with his mouth. He felt himself harden as she sighed against his lips.

'Ahem.'

Charlie froze. He'd know that disapproving noise anywhere. Carrie pressed desperately against him to get away. 'I really need a lock on that door,' he announced loudly enough for his father to hear.

'Maybe a little self-control wouldn't go astray, either.'

Charlie made sure Carrie was together and smiled at her before he turned around. 'Hello, Father.'

Oh, God! Mr Wentworth, Charlie's father, eminent thoracic surgeon, had caught them necking like a pair of horny teenagers.

'Charles.'

'This is Carrie,' Charlie said calmly.

'Who is just leaving,' Carrie said, her legs shaking as she made a quick escape.

At Friday lunchtime Carrie was sitting at the table, trying to concentrate on a bunch of exceedingly boring, exceedingly depressing figures. *Damn it.* The hospital board was going to have a field day. The centre wasn't viable. The previous year's figures were a mess. She knew she would have to make a recommendation to the board that would destroy Charlie and his beloved centre.

And their so-called friendship. And most definitely their snogging. After she delivered her verdict she was pretty sure he'd never want to see her again—never mind kiss her.

It was developing into a true conflict of interest for her. She was torn. Torn between what the figures told her, the black and white, and what she knew about Charlie and his goals and aims for the centre—the grey.

A few weeks ago she'd been nothing but a bottom-line girl. A black and white girl. But the longer she spent at the centre and witnessed the difference Charlie and the centre made, she knew she couldn't be objective. She had gone to the grey side.

She threw down her pen and glared at the stack of paperwork in front of her. The jukebox thumped away in the background and somewhere outside a car backfired. How the hell was she going to tell him?

Maybe this was an easy out for her? This crazy passion-fuelled supposed friendship they had now couldn't go on. Their issues hadn't changed. Her time there was almost up. If she left, putting the final nail in the centre's coffin, it would achieve what they'd so far not managed to achieve. The end of their impossible, never-going-to-happen relationship.

Carrie was still musing over the problem a couple of minutes later when Angela burst through the door.

'I need you. Now. I have a GSW outside.'

Carrie startled at the receptionist's abrupt entry and rapid-fire demand. A gunshot wound? *Oh, no!* She stood on shaky legs. 'Get Charlie.'

Angela glared at her impatiently. 'Do you think I'd be here, asking you, if Charlie was around?'

Good point. She watched Angela's brisk retreat.

'Stat,' Angela bellowed from down the hallway.

Carrie jumped, her heart leaping in her chest. Her legs responded to the brisk command, her thoughts jumbled as she felt the familiar edge of panic.

She entered the treatment room, nausea slamming into her gut at the bloodied victim.

'Shotgun blast to the abdomen,' Angela said, thrusting a pair of gloves at her. 'That car backfiring earlier was not a car backfiring. The ambulance is eight minutes out.'

The patient looked like a teenager. He had an oxygen mask on and was writhing around the examination bed, holding his abdomen. Blood was oozing out all over his hands, and its metallic aroma wafted towards her, fuelling even more nausea. It was all over his clothes and the clean white sheets. *Oh, God, why wasn't Charlie here? Where the hell was he?*

Another teenager was pacing in the corner. He had blood all over his clothes, too. 'Help him. Don't just stand there. Help him,' he yelled at Carrie, running his bloodied hands through his hair.

Angela looked at her sternly. They were it. *She* was it. She was what stood between this boy and death. Did she want another boy to bleed and die before her eyes?

Her thoughts crystallised. Her thinking became ordered. *D.R.A.B.C.H.*

The first four letters checked out already. There was no danger, the boy was obviously responsive and, at a quick glance, his airway and breathing weren't compromised. She noticed a blood-pressure cuff wrapped around his arm and a pulse oximeter attached to his finger.

She strode closer. 'What's his pressure?'

'Eighty systolic,' Angela returned quickly. 'Heart rate one-twenty. Sats ninety-eight per cent.'

Carrie nodded. 'I'll get some lines in. Have we got a plasma expander?'

Angela nodded as she pushed the IV trolley towards her. 'I'll set up two Haemaccel lines.'

Carrie snapped on a tourniquet. Her hand trembled as she attempted and gained access to a vein in the crook of the teenager's elbow. In trauma situations these veins were the most commonly used. They were big, allowing a decent-sized cannulae to be placed for rapid infusion of large amounts of fluid, and were generally easy to find.

Angela taped it in place while Carrie moved around to the other side and placed one in the opposite arm. In a few minutes they had two litres of fluid running into the patient. 'Pressure?'

'Ninety systolic.'

Improving, but there was no way of telling just how much blood their patient had lost or was continuing to lose. Carrie turned her attention to the wound. There was a large hole in the abdominal wall, with loops of bowel protruding. Blood oozed out continuously. Where exactly it was coming from was anyone's guess. In all probability there could be multiple sites. Bowel, kidney, liver, stomach. And that wasn't even counting the threat to major blood vessels.

'He needs a laparotomy,' Carrie said. There could also be spinal complications although, given the boy's powerful thrashing, everything appeared intact.

Angela nodded. 'In the meantime, let's put some moist packs in the hole to protect the exposed bowel. The ambulance should be here in a couple of minutes.'

Angela opened a pre-packaged trauma pack and poured sterile saline onto the large white hanky-sized sponges. Carrie snapped on the sterile gloves Angela opened and placed two of them over the hole, gently tucking them inside.

'Pressure?' Carrie asked as she watched the packs turn red instantly.

'Holding at ninety,' Angela confirmed. 'Here, put this sterile towel over the wound.' Angela passed her a sterile green towel. Carrie draped the hole and Angela taped the towel to the skin.

'Pity we don't carry any S8s. He could do with some pain relief,' Angela commented over the loud moans of the patient's distress.

Carrie nodded. That was one of the many proposals in Charlie's expansion plans for the centre. The ones she was going to dash. 'His blood pressure's probably a little dicey anyway.'

The wailing of a siren grew louder and Carrie realised she'd been so focused on stabilising the teenager that she'd tuned everything else out. She'd been like a machine. Like she'd been doing this all her life. Like she'd never stopped.

'I'll direct them in,' Angela said, removing her gloves.

Charlie was a hundred metres away when the ambulance whizzed passed him, its siren blaring, and braked outside the drop-in centre. He threw his sandwich in a nearby bin and ran. *What the hell had happened?*

He skidded to a halt as Angela emerged from the centre. 'What happened?' he demanded.

'Gunshot wound to the abdomen,' Angela told him calmly.

'Carrie?'

Angela nodded. 'Handled it like a pro.' She turned to brief the paramedics walking with them inside as she spoke.

He burst into the treatment room. Carrie had her back to the door and a stethoscope in her ears and didn't hear him enter.

Charlie touched her shoulder. 'Carrie?'

She turned. 'Oh…hi. Blood pressure's up to one hundred,' she said, diverting her gaze from Charlie's worried face to the paramedics striding through the door.

Charlie stood back and watched in awe as Carrie gave a concise handover. 'I think he's just a scoop and go, guys. He's going to need Theatre, stat. He's actively bleeding in there somewhere.'

Five minutes later they had the patient loaded and were departing. Angela, Charlie and Carrie watched it disappear from view.

'Good job, Dr Douglas,' Angela said as she turned and headed back into the clinic.

Carrie stared after her, open-mouthed. *Dr Douglas?*

Charlie whistled. 'High praise, indeed, *Dr* Douglas.'

Carrie shielded her eyes from the bright sunlight as she looked up into his face. It seemed she had come full circle in Angela's eyes. In Charlie's eyes. She had earned her stripes. Earned herself the right to the title Doctor. She had saved the teenager's life.

'Are you OK?' he asked.

Carrie thought about it for a moment. Remarkably, she was. In fact, the thrill of having taken control and saved her patient's life was elating. Pushing papers around a desk never gave her this kind of buzz. She nodded. 'Yes, I am, actually. I haven't felt this OK for a long time.'

Charlie smiled. He lifted his hand and stroked his knuckles down her cheek. He pulled her into his shoulder for a lingering hug. 'Come on,' he said, his arm around her as he moved inside. 'You'd better go and change your shirt.'

Carrie looked down and noticed a blood stain the size of a grapefruit on her silky purple blouse. She should have worn an apron.

'I can help you with that if you like,' he murmured.

Carrie smiled and then stopped, her euphoria fading as she remembered that she was about to put Charlie out of business. 'Thanks. I can manage.'

Carrie opened the staffroom door and wandered over to the table. Her laptop hummed quietly, a stack of papers waiting for her attention next to it. She picked the top sheet up and looked at it. A bank reconciliation.

'Here you go,' Charlie said from halfway down the hallway. 'It's not silk and it'll be miles too big, but it'll do.'

Carrie accepted the shirt without even glancing at it. She sat down at the table.

'Are you OK?' he asked. She was quiet suddenly and seemed pensive. Was it a delayed reaction? Was she about to hyperventilate?

'I don't want to do this any more.' Carrie picked up another sheet of paper and tossed it in the air. She wished she hadn't taken this job. But, then, she never would have met Charlie. Never would have had her eyes open to the fact that she was doctor. Not a manager.

Charlie's eyes followed the lazy fall of the paper. What did she mean? 'Careful. I know the lady that owns them and they're probably in order.'

Carrie smiled. 'It felt amazing just now. I mean, I was terrified to start with, I was frantic to have you by my side, but…we were it. Me and Angela. And I couldn't let another boy die. And it all came back to me.'

'It wasn't your fault, Carrie. The other boy. He was taken away from the hospital before you had a chance to examine him properly.'

She nodded. 'I know that…I do, really, but…I've had that image of him in my head for so long now. The white sheets…the red blood…his dead-looking eyes. But today's changed everything. I have a new image. Of me. As a doctor. I know I certainly can't go back to this.' Carrie placed her hand on the paperwork.

Charlie felt a surge of relief wash over him. He'd always known there was a doctor inside her, fighting to get out. 'Bravo.' He smiled. 'I know a certain drop-in centre that desperately needs a female doctor. Especially one who's good with figures.'

Carrie felt her heart slam against her ribs. Her fingers felt dead and heavy suddenly against the pile of paper. He had offered her something she'd wanted since childhood and had convinced herself it hadn't mattered that she hadn't had it—a gig in community medicine.

Tell him. She should tell him. He'd given her the perfect opportunity. But she couldn't. Not today. She'd just saved a life and she didn't want to besmirch it with bottom-line stuff.

'I may just take you up on that.'

CHAPTER NINE

CARRIE drove to the clinic on Monday morning knowing that today was the day. It wasn't fair to put it off any longer. She'd been over and over the figures all weekend and no matter how much she tried to present them in a good light, the truth was inescapable. The Valley Drop-In Centre was not financially viable.

It gave her a chill, just thinking about it. Charlie would be devastated. The centre was everything to him. She was so not looking forward to the conversation she needed to have with him first thing this morning.

Part of her wanted to chicken out. Leave the dirty work up to the board. Have the news arrive in one of those awful official yellow envelopes. But she knew she owed him more than that.

She couldn't believe how much could change in a few short weeks. How much this assignment had affected her entire life. Before coming to the centre, she wouldn't have thought twice about getting rid of something that wasn't performing. It was, after all, taxpayers' money they were playing with, entrusted with—serious stuff. And it wasn't their place to waste it willy-nilly.

But trying to justify a venture like this on paper just didn't take into account the human aspect. What the centre meant to the community it supported and what it would mean if it wasn't around any longer. Whatever happened, she was going to make sure she stressed that in her final report.

But the real reason it was ripping her heart out was much more depressing. She had fallen in love with Charlie. The revelation had come last night as she'd been putting Dana to bed. Her daughter had hugged her and whispered, 'I wish Charlie could be my daddy.'

And it had hit her. She wished he could be, too. Wished it had been Charlie and not Rupert who had fathered Dana. The truth had only depressed her further. She loved him. She wanted him by her side. Always. In her bed. In her life. In her heart.

She shook herself as she stopped at a red light. Why? Why had she risked her heart on someone else who was reluctant to be a father to Dana? She'd never asked to feel like this. Never expected to feel like this. Didn't want to feel like this.

Since everything had fallen apart five years ago she hadn't even entertained such fanciful expectations. She'd had Dana, who gave her indescribable joy, and her career. Work, Dana, work, Dana. It may have been soulless but she'd been… content.

Maybe she'd just settled as a way to punish herself for Harry's death or for her naïvety over Rupert. Maybe it had been a way of protecting herself from further emotional trauma. Whatever it was, Charlie had turned it all upside down. He'd given her back her soul.

But more than that, he had given medicine back to her. The excitement she'd once felt at the prospect of helping sick people get better, of improving their quality of life or helping them to a dignified death. The thrill that came with the power to heal. The joy of knowing she was making a difference. No matter what happened after this morning, she was trading in her pinstripes for a white coat.

She parked her car as a swirl of emotions whirled in her head. A part of her wanted to throw caution to the wind and rush in head first. But the lessons of Rupert weren't easily forgotten and she knew she had to be more responsible this time. It wasn't just her future, her fate she had to decide on. There was an innocent four-year-old also involved.

Of course, after today it was probably all going to be moot anyway. Things seemed fairly insurmountable at the moment. Even if they did somehow manage to get past her part in the centre's closure, there was the issue of Dana.

She couldn't force Charlie to be a father to her daughter and he seemed to have it in his head that he wasn't up to the job. Parental influences could be powerful and far-reaching—half the centre's runaways were a perfect example of how not to parent. But it was obvious to anyone with the slightest vision that he was a natural with kids.

So how could she convince him he wasn't like his father? And how, after her bombshell today, could she convince him to even listen?

Carrie heard voices from Charlie's office as she swung by and she felt tension twist her stomach into another knot. She wanted to be anywhere but here today, doing this. She stood in front of his door, took a deep breath and poised her hand to knock.

'Charles, you're not seriously involved with that Carrie girl, are you?'

Carrie stopped before her knuckles hit the wood. His door wasn't completely pulled to and she could hear the conversation easily. Was Charlie's father with him?

'What makes you think that?' Charlie bounced a rubber ball against the wall as he lounged back in his chair. It hit the floor, hit the wall and returned to him in a perfect arc.

He'd learnt a long time ago to tune out during one of his father's phone calls. Don't react, don't supply him with any ammunition—just say yes and no and give noncommittal grunts in the right places and get the hell off the line as fast as possible.

'You missed Sunday lunch. Your mother was most upset.'

Charlie smiled. Playing hookey was the only thing that had improved his mood over the weekend. It had given him a brief respite from thoughts of Carrie. 'Sorry.'

Carrie dropped her hand and leaned closer. No, she thought, there was too much of an echo. Charlie must have him on speakerphone.

'You know she has an illegitimate child? That's not really something we encourage in the Wentworth family.'

Carrie blinked. Illegitimate? Did anyone seriously use that word any more? Did anyone seriously care any more? She was beginning to see why Charlie and his father didn't get on.

Charlie grimaced. Pompous ass. He was doing exactly what Charlie had known he'd do. Stick his nose into Carrie's background to check out her pedigree. 'She's a friend, Dad, that's all.' Bounce. Bounce.

Carrie sucked in a breath. She was surprised how much Charlie's dismissal of their relationship hurt. It shouldn't, that's what they'd agreed, after all. She should be happy that he was trying to stick to their deal. But the deal had come before her revelation. She knew now she could never just be friends with Charlie Wentworth.

'You know Veronica was asking after you the other day?'

Carrie swallowed. She should stop. This was a private conversation and none of her business. But, try as she may, she couldn't drag herself away.

'Oh, yes?' Charlie stifled a yawn. Bounce. Bounce.

Carrie felt her breath catch in her throat. *He was interested?*

'Said she missed you.'

Bounce. Bounce. Charlie rolled his eyes. *Hell—kill me now.* 'Really?' He'd rather go without sex for another year.

Carrie swallowed. He *was* interested. There was a pain in her chest. He wanted his ex back?

'Play your cards right and I'm sure she'd take you back.'

'Really?' Charlie said distractedly. Thoughts of sex had reminded him of how he had peeled Carrie's clothes off with his teeth last weekend. Bounce. Bounce.

Carrie ordered herself to breathe. Which she did. She ordered herself to move. Which she did not. The conversation was horribly fascinating—like a motorway smash, gruesome but compelling.

'What is that infernal noise, Charles?'

Charlie had had just about enough of the conversation. 'Someone knocking at my door.' *I do work, Daddy, Dearest.* 'My first appointment for the day. I'd better go.' Bounce. Bounce.

'So you'll apply for that surgical position, then?'

'No.' Charlie ended the call, pleased to have it over and done with. He checked his watch as he rose from his desk. Carrie was late. Maybe if he lurked by his doorway he could lure her inside.

He opened his door and jumped as he came face to face with her. The look on her face told him she had heard everything.

'Hi,' he said.

'Hi.'

'You heard that, didn't you?'

Carrie nodded.

Charlie couldn't tell what she was thinking. Her gaze seemed blank. She looked kind of frozen. That wasn't good. 'It probably didn't sound too good from your side of the door.'

He reached out to touch her, to tell her it wasn't what she'd thought, but she drew back.

Carrie felt her brain power up. 'No…it's fine. I'm sorry, I shouldn't have been listening. It was none of my business.'

It was good that she'd overheard. To know that he hadn't really got over his ex-wife. It made the conversation they had to have easier. It made their parting easier. And it didn't matter that her heart was breaking. It was better to know now where she really stood in his life. Before she had too long to get used to loving him. Better to know before Dana got involved, too.

'Let me explain,' he said, taking another step towards her.

'Charlie, really,' Carrie said briskly. 'This is unimportant. There's something much more pressing I need to discuss with you.' She turned on her heel and headed straight for the staff-room, placing her laptop on the table.

She paced while she waited for him. She hummed a nursery rhyme in her head, determined not to think about the conversation she'd just overheard. About her fledgling love being well and truly flattened. She had to get through this. Afterwards she could fall apart. She could cry and rail against the fates. Right now she had work to do.

Charlie entered and she looked at him and couldn't decide what she wanted to do more—run to him or slap his face.

'Shut the door,' she ordered.

OK. This was bad. And he didn't think it was about the phone call. She looked serious. Deadly serious. Her pin-stripes had never looked primmer. He turned and did her bidding then faced her.

'You're closing the centre down.'

Carrie suppressed a gasp. She could see his jaw clench and unclench and guessed the calmness of his statement had cost him a lot.

She swallowed. 'The centre is not viable. It will be my recommendation to the board that closure is the most expedient course of action.'

Charlie felt the burn of anger scorch his chest. 'Expedient.'

Carrie flinched at the disgust in his voice. He repeated it as if it was the dirtiest word in the dictionary. She lifted her chin. 'Yes. Expedient.' *To hell with him.*

'I thought you'd changed. I thought you'd started to see past the bottom line.'

His barb hit home. *He knew she had.* She had changed so much in her time there. But that didn't alter the facts. 'My job is to look after the hospital's money.'

Charlie strode to the door and whipped it open. He pointed to the teenagers that were already lining up for their first game of pool. 'What are these kids going to do? Where are they going to go?'

'That data is not required by the board—'

'Data?' he interrupted furiously, slamming the door closed. 'They're people!'

Carrie swallowed. 'Rest assured, as with any report, I will also state the reasons against closure, which will include those issues.' *Dear God, she sounded so pompous. So bureaucratic.*

Charlie couldn't believe what he was hearing. The centre was the heart and soul of this needy community. He couldn't allow this to happen. It was madness. 'Is this because of us?'

It took a brief moment for the full implications of his statement to sink in. 'I beg your pardon?'

'Well, let's see. You haven't mentioned a word to me once about the state of play and then this morning you overhear a phone call and now you're shutting me down?'

Carrie felt herself stiffen. 'I resent your inference. This was a professional investigation. What happened between us privately has absolutely no bearing on the outcome.'

'You sure there isn't a little vengeance in there, Carrie?'

She stared at him, at his indignation, and her heart ached. But she didn't need to stick around and be insulted. Have her integrity called into question. She'd been down that road once in her professional career and had barely survived. She wasn't about to let Charlie do it to her all over again.

She picked up her laptop and fished around in her pocket for the locker key he had given her the first day. 'You will be receiving official notification in due course.'

Charlie rubbed a hand through his hair and stared at the key dangling from her outstretched fingers. This was making him crazy. First his father and then this? It was too much for one morning. She looked so self-righteous. So businesslike.

What did tie-dye Carrie think of it? Didn't this bombshell affect her at all?

'There'll be an outcry. This centre will close over my dead body,' he warned.

She hoped so, she really did. But the words wouldn't come. This conversation had dealt the fatal blow to their relationship…friendship…kissing-buddy thingy—whatever the hell it was. As hard as it was, it was necessary for them to both move on. He had a chance with his ex and she had a life with Dana to get on with.

She went for a nonchalant shrug. 'That's not my concern. Goodbye, Charlie. I hope you and Veronica are very happy.'

The light flippant delivery cost her dearly. She walked past him, her head held high, her back erect, her fingers squeezing the laptop bag handle with a death-like grip. She didn't want to go. But she couldn't stay, either.

Charlie watched Carrie disappear and realised the awful truth. She was ruining him twice. She wasn't only going to take the centre away but she'd also walked away with his heart. He had fallen in love with her.

It had crept up on him unawares but it was there nonetheless. No wonder he hadn't been able to stop thinking about her. No wonder the women at the club the other night had left him cold. He'd been fooling himself that it was lust—a combination of pinstripes and abstinence. But as she walked away and an intense pain ripped through his gut, he knew it was deeper than that. Much deeper.

Deeper than anything he'd ever felt before. Sure, he'd loved Veronica but, looking back, he wasn't so sure he'd liked her very much. His father had liked her so that should have been a clue from the start. And to finally have his father's approval had definitely helped keep the thing between them going.

But Carrie was different. She had facets to her character that Veronica had never had. And he loved each one. The businesswoman, the re-emerging doctor, the generous lover, the devoted mother. She was multi-dimensional and complex and he couldn't bear the thought of living his life without her.

His feelings were so intense that not even her proposal to shut the centre, to tear his heart out, could dampen them. Now he'd opened the floodgates, his love was gushing through his system unabated. Not that admitting it helped. It seemed today, more than ever, their problems were completely insurmountable.

He pulled up a chair and sank into it. Hell—it wasn't even eight o'clock yet!

Two days passed. Two long, slow, agonising days. Charlie relived their last words over and over. He relived the phone call from his father over and over. Every damning word. Her glib 'I hope you and Veronica are happy' rang in his ears.

He wished she'd given him the chance to explain. She hadn't had the benefit of years of similar conversations with his father. She didn't know the best way to deal with them was to tune them out. He'd hardly been paying attention for most of it. But his words came back at him repeatedly. His noncommittal replies. His bored tone. His evasive comebacks. None of that inflection, the grimacing, the rolled eyes would have been obvious from the other side of the door. No wonder she thought he was interested in his ex.

Between that and exploring avenues to keep the centre open he'd had plenty on his mind. He rubbed his hands through his hair. He felt like he had after Donny had first stabbed him with the syringe. Powerless. In limbo all over again. His options removed. His freedom denied.

He stood and paced around his desk. No. *No more.* Hadn't he decided just last week that he was reclaiming his life? That he wasn't going to wait around any longer? Carrie had challenged him to get a life and he'd taken her up on that. Was he really going to let circumstances block him again?

It had taken him a long time to build up the centre. To gain the trust of locals and authorities alike. And it had taken him for ever to find his soul mate. And he'd be damned if he was going to give up on either of them without a fight.

Two things he knew for sure. He wanted the centre and he wanted Carrie. The thought of being a father to Dana was completely terrifying, but he knew Carrie's daughter had wormed her way into his affections, despite his concerns, and he wanted to be a part of her life, too. A part of both of their lives.

OK, Carrie didn't love him. Yet. And he knew he'd be foolish to push that. That she would need time to be certain of his love for her and Dana. And slow would be good to ease into a relationship with Dana. If they took things slowly, maybe the prospect of being a father wouldn't be so daunting?

But he had to be let in first. He may have only known her for a short time, but her goodbye had seemed very final to him. He paced a bit more, trying to think of a way to reach out to her.

It came to him a few moments later. *Of course.* The centre. She was good with figures and she knew the financial state of his workplace much better than he did. Surely she'd be interested in helping him to find a way to make it work? No, scratch that—more than make it work. He wanted to go grander. He wanted the expansion, damn it!

OK—she'd been sent here to do a job. And she'd done it. But was it how she really felt deep down? If he'd been a betting man, he would have wagered against it. Surely, with her own personal journey back to medicine so intimately linked with the centre, she could be persuaded to help?

He picked up the phone and dialled her home number without giving himself time to change her mind. A young woman answered.

'Hi, you must be Susie. This is Charlie.'

'Ah, Charlie. Dana talks about you non-stop.'

Charlie smiled. Nice to know he was in one of the Douglas women's good books. 'Is Carrie in?'

''Fraid not. She and Dana are spending a few days at her mum's place.'

'Oh, right…OK, then. If you hear from her, tell her I called.'

Charlie replaced the phone in the cradle. *Damn it!* What now? He had to see her. It had been two days and he was going mad without her. He rose from his desk and stalked out of his office. The area was deserted and the jukebox was blissfully silent.

He sat in Angela's chair at the reception desk and opened the bottom drawer, reaching for the phone book. He flipped through the pages until he came to the 'D' section then thumbed through, locating Douglases. Carrie had mentioned last weekend the suburb where her parents lived.

Charlie found four Douglases listed and prayed that Carrie's parents were one of them. He'd grabbed his stuff and locked up the centre. He would visit each address until he found her. He started the Datsun and prayed they didn't have an unlisted number.

Carrie was grateful, as she sat beside her mother, that her father had volunteered to bath Dana tonight. Her heart had been so heavy the last few days that any help getting through the day was appreciated. Coming to her parents' had been a good idea. It was a distraction for Dana, whose incessant chatter about Charlie was heartbreaking. And a distraction for her, too. Someone to talk with to take her mind off being in love with someone who didn't love her back.

Her mother put her arm around Carrie's shoulders and the brave demeanour Carrie had been putting on since she'd arrived cracked into a thousand pieces. 'Why, Mum? Why? I should never have got involved.'

'Oh, darling.' Meryl Douglas stroked her daughter's fringe. 'We don't get to choose if or who we fall in love with.'

'Dana's going to hate me,' Carrie wailed, dissolving into tears. 'She adores him.'

Carrie despised herself for this weakness. After Rupert she'd vowed she'd never cry over another man and here she was, five years older but obviously not any wiser. Damn Charlie. Damn him to hell. It wasn't fair to worm his way into her life, wake her from her sleep, show her a better existence and then deny her the right to claim it.

Charlie pulled up at the fourth residence not at all confident that he'd have any luck here, either. The house was a typical Brisbane champher-board, high-set house. It was plain, nondescript, the paint a little worn in places. But it was neat, the grass clipped short, garden beds decorating the fence borders. An ancient-looking, floppy-eared Irish setter adorning the bottom step hobbled towards him as he pushed open the gate. It sniffed the hand that Charlie offered and licked it.

'Hello, there, boy,' Charlie crooned, scratching the sweet spot behind the dog's ear. 'Is Carrie here?'

The dog looked at him myopically and Charlie chuckled.

He took a deep breath, climbed the steps two at a time and knocked on the door. His blood pounded through his ears.

The door opened. 'Charlie!'

Charlie looked down to see Dana's adorable face staring back at him. She'd obviously not long had a bath as her hair was damp and she was in her tie-dye pyjamas. She threw herself at him, wrapping her arms around his leg. Charlie felt his heart would burst it swelled with so much love for the little blonde-haired, blue-eyed cherub who had captivated him from the very beginning. He reached down and picked her up, settling her on his hip.

'I missed you, Charlie.'

'I missed you, too, Sleeping Beauty.'

'Dana?'

A woman who must have been Carrie's mother approached. They had the same hair and the same whiskey-coloured eyes.

'Granny, this is Charlie.'

Charlie felt the lump in his throat grow bigger. Dana had introduced him like he was Superman, and he knew he would leap tall buildings for the daughter of the woman he loved. Could he be a good father to her? Her trusting eyes made him believe he could.

'Hello, Mrs Douglas,' Charlie said politely.

'I take it you'd like to see Carrie?'

Charlie could see the reticence in the older woman's eyes but he could also see an innate kindness. He nodded. 'Very much.'

'Come in.'

Charlie breathed a sigh of relief as Carrie's mother stood aside and allowed him to enter. Dana clung to his neck and jiggled around in his arms.

He was led into a lounge room. 'Come on, Dana, sweetie. Bedtime.'

Dana protested and Charlie passed her over to her grandmother reluctantly. 'I want Charlie to read to me.' Dana pouted.

'Another day, Sleeping Beauty.' Charlie shot Dana his most reassuring smile. If he had his way, he'd be reading to her every night.

'Promise, Charlie?'

Dana looked so earnest and he crossed his fingers behind his back. 'Promise.'

Dana and her grandmother left the room and for the first time he noticed Carrie standing in the doorway. He wanted to run to her but she looked distant, her arms crossed, everything about her discouraging any familiarities.

'Don't do that. You'll only build her hopes up. You shouldn't make promises you can't keep.'

Charlie swallowed. 'I'd like to be able to keep it.'

'I thought you didn't want to be a father to a four-year-old?'

'Carrie…let me explain.'

'Don't waste your breath, Charlie. Save it for Veronica.'

'Damn it, Carrie,' Charlie swore, striding towards her. 'I don't want Veronica. I only want you.'

He was right in front of her now. Close. So close she could almost touch him. And she wanted to. She'd not seen him for two whole days and the potency of his presence was lethal. She pushed away from the doorframe and took care not to brush against him as she moved into the room, away from his intoxicating nearness.

He turned to face her. 'I know how it must have sounded the other day.'

Carrie gave a bitter laugh. 'Really?'

Charlie sighed. 'You have to understand how it is with my father and I. We have a fraught relationship. I didn't turn out to be what he wanted. My rebellion had always stuck in his craw. So I endure dinner with my parents every Sunday and he rings every week to chew my ear about something I've done that's disappointed him. I guess you can say it's the price I pay for walking my own path.'

Despite her animosity towards him, Charlie painted a bleak portrait of his family life. She almost felt sorry for him. No wonder he doubted his ability to parent. No wonder he had enjoyed his time in her home so much. She couldn't imagine not having the support of her parents. They'd always been behind her in everything she'd done.

'I usually just tune him out. Take the phone call because otherwise he rings incessantly and then I have Angela on my case. He prattles on about my divorce and a surgical position he could get me and I barely even listen. I just say yes, no, really, maybe and grunt a lot.'

Carrie sighed. She didn't want to know this. She didn't want to listen to this. She wanted him gone. Before she did something stupid, like throw herself at him.

'I really don't want to rehash this, Charlie. If that's what you came for, you might as well just leave now.'

Charlie could see the dark smudges under her eyes. She looked tired, like she hadn't been sleeping. Now, that he could relate to. She looked like she was out of patience and he knew that trying to convince her of his love tonight was the wrong move.

'I want you to help me save the centre.'

'What?'

Bingo! 'Have you completed your report?'

'Today.'

'Have you submitted it?'

She shook her head. 'Tomorrow.' *Along with my resignation.*

'Don't.'

Carrie shot him an exasperated look. 'I hope you didn't come to persuade me to interfere with my investigation.' *I love you but I won't do that.*

'No.' He shook his head vehemently. 'Of course not. I'm just asking you to…delay it a little.'

'Charlie…'

'No.' He put his hands up in a silencing gesture. 'Just hear me out, OK? You know the centre's finances backwards. You know how it got broken. You must know how it can be fixed. I have a bunch of ideas I've been working on—' he thrust a folder towards her '—to make the expansion and the clinic viable. And I know you can do the rest.'

'Charlie…' she pleaded. She just wanted to get on with her life. She didn't want any more involvement with him. It would be hard enough loving him and never seeing him again. But having to work with him to save the centre? She'd never survive it.

'I know you care about the centre. You go on about the bottom line but I've seen the change in you over the last few weeks. And the centre did that. It gave you back your love of medicine.'

Carrie felt tears well in her eyes. 'No, Charlie. You gave me back my love of medicine.'

He shrugged. 'I am the centre.'

She nodded. He was right. Every patient, every basketball game, every ding in the walls was his. He'd built it up. His personal stamp was everywhere. Every corner, every piece of furniture had a story. And he could relay each one.

'I know you care what happens to my community. To people. I could see that in you that night you knelt on the road beside me.'

He walked towards her slowly until he was so close he could hear her uneven breathing. He stroked a hand down the side of her neck and rubbed his thumb over the pulse that was beating frantically at the base of her throat.

'You were scared rigid but you helped anyway. I need your help again, Carrie.'

She swallowed. The man she loved was standing before her, touching her, asking her for something. Did she have the power to deny him? *My community*, he had said. His community. Could she turn her back on a bunch of people who needed Charlie and his centre? People who in a few short weeks had managed to also enter her affections?

'I'll look…' She stopped and coughed to clear the huskiness from her voice. 'Look over it and let you know.'

She took a step back and relieved him of the folder.

'Thank you.'

Carrie nodded, not trusting her voice. He reached out for her and she took another step back, shaking her head, impossibly weary. He had to go before she completely broke down. Because then he might hold her and she couldn't be responsible for her actions if he touched her. She was trying to salvage as much pride out of this as she could—he didn't need to see her impersonation of a raving wreck.

'Goodbye, Charlie.'

She turned and left the lounge room, uncaring about how or if he left. She just had to get away before she crumpled. Before she laid her head against his chest and begged him to love her. Love them.

She wandered into her old bedroom. Dana was fast asleep on a portable bed, all snug and safe. One blonde lock covering an eye. Her daughter was going to be heartbroken.

'Damn you, Charlie. Damn you for making us love you.'

Carrie felt like someone had put red-hot pokers in her eyes the next morning. She'd been up until four a.m., going over the ideas that Charlie had given her and considering them in context with the centre's current financial woes. Charlie had been right when he'd said she'd know how to fix it. But she'd been impressed with his thoughts and she'd felt a buzz of excitement and possibility course through her bloodstream, which had kept her awake despite her tiredness.

The potential and possibilities for the centre were enormous. But it needed a lot of TLC and someone who had both medical and administration skills. Charlie was hopeless. He was a fantastic doctor, a caring and dedicated advocate for the community. But his business acumen sucked. In short, the centre needed someone just like her! *Not her.* Someone *like* her.

She clicked on the 'print' icon on her computer screen and yawned as she waited for the multi-paged document to spit out of the machine beneath her desk. It was her report. Her altered report. It encompassed the problems but also the solutions and Charlie's grand plans to make it a facility that would do Brisbane proud. She would take it to Charlie and then she would submit it to the board.

She opened another document and clicked on the 'print' icon again. A copy of her resignation was in her hands in a matter of seconds. She looked it over. Fear and uncertainty grasped at her gut. But as she folded it to fit into a sterile yellow envelope she knew she was doing the right thing. This job was slowly strangling her. She knew that now. Thanks to Charlie and the centre. She was ready to go back to the coalface.

She passed the boardroom on her way to the medical director's office, envelope in hand. She felt strangely compelled to enter. On this, her last day, she needed to confront a few ghosts.

She looked around at the rich, elegant décor. She inhaled and the smell of leather and wood assaulted her nostrils. Before her current assignment this room had always given her goose-bumps. There was something strangely seductive about the management nerve centre. The room where all the decisions were made. The power was almost tangible. She had known the minute she'd set foot in it that this was her destiny.

Now the room was stifling. Oppressive. The thought of sitting at this table and talking policies and strategic planning left her empty. She left quickly, wanting no reminder of the mistake she'd nearly made, thinking that this was her path in life. If nothing else, and despite her broken heart, she had Charlie to thank for removing her blinkers.

She strode purposefully to her boss's office. He wasn't in. She placed the yellow envelope on his desk, where he couldn't fail to see it when he returned. And then turned around and walked out of the hospital. Today was a new beginning for her. Her personal life may have been a mess but her medical career was finally back on track.

Charlie was in his office, talking to Joe, when Carrie arrived.

'Hi, Joe.'

'Hey, Carrie.' He winked. 'We've missed you around here.'

Carrie nodded distractedly, her eyes barely acknowledging him as she sought the one pair of eyes she'd come there for.

'Hello, Charlie.'

Charlie stood up, encouraged by the shimmer in her whiskey-coloured depths. 'Hi.'

They stood staring at each other hungrily for a few moments. She at the door, he at his desk. Joe rolled his eyes and gave Carrie a gentle push inside, closing the door and shutting them away in a bubble of privacy.

Carrie smiled and took a step forward. 'I looked over your ideas.' She threw the document on the table. 'I think we can save the clinic. This is the report that I plan on submitting later this afternoon.'

Charlie's heart beat frantically and his hand shook slightly as he picked up the wad of paper.

'It will take some streamlining. Some adjustment in the way you run things. It certainly involves employing a practice manager. But I think, with the help of some hefty private-sector support, it can be done.'

Carrie paced as she talked in the small space available. She slipped into businesswoman mode, more nervous than she'd ever been at how he would take it.

Charlie's heartbeat accelerated as he flicked through the report. It was comprehensive and substantive. She must have been up all night.

'Did you sleep last night?'

Carrie gave a wry smile. 'A little.'

It was marvellous. Charlie knew he held in his hands the ability to keep the centre going. And Carrie had given him the way. 'It's amazing! I don't know what to say...how to thank you.'

He rounded the desk and before either of them could caution against it swept her into his arms, enfolding her in a warm embrace.

Carrie hung on, most definitely swept away. This was where she belonged. How unfair was life?

The door barged open and they sprang apart guiltily. 'Charles! What is the meaning of this?' Ignatius Wentworth demanded.

Carrie froze and looked from father to son. She could see all the veins standing out in Charlie's father's neck. But Charlie looked pretty angry also, a nerve twitching at the angle of his jaw. She edged closer to him.

'Exactly what it looks like,' Charlie said calmly, gathering Carrie to his side and placing an arm around her back, his hand resting on her shoulder.

Ignatius looked from one to the other. 'I thought you were just friends. You can't be serious.'

'Perfectly.' Charlie smiled down at the woman he loved and stroked the skin at her nape.

'But…Veronica.'

'We're divorced.'

'You can get her back.'

Charlie laughed. 'I don't want her back. I want Carrie.'

Carrie's heart thundered as Charlie's father gave her a once-over.

'You want to be a father to another man's child? Preposterous!'

The slow stroke of Charlie's thumb on her neck was reassuring and she lifted her chin and looked Ignatius Wentworth straight in the eye.

'I would be Dana's father with pride.'

Carrie looked at him, startled. Was he just saying that to annoy his father? He looked dead serious.

'You can do better than this.'

Charlie felt a flare of anger scorch his cheeks and burn in his stomach. His finger stilled its rhythmic movement. 'I would be very, very careful what you say, Father.'

Carrie shivered at the steel she heard in Charlie's voice. She saw surprise register in the older man's eyes, replaced with a slightly bewildered look.

'Charles…please. You could be a top-class surgeon. Have a brilliant career. Why are you wasting your life down here with these people? You could have your choice of specialties.'

Carrie cleared her throat. What was wrong with this oaf? Couldn't he see that what Charlie did *was* a specialty?

'With all due respect, Dr Wentworth, community medicine *is* a specialty and a very worthwhile one, too.' Carrie's voice was shaky and Charlie's father was looking at her like she'd just answered the headmaster back.

She pushed on anyway. 'And your son is a brilliant doctor. He may not cut open chests or find cures for cancer, but he's the life force in this community. He's the man these people come to if they're sick, if they're dying, if they're beaten, if they're in trouble, if they've got nowhere to sleep and nothing to eat or even if they've just lost their way. He's got grand plans for this place and he's just the visionary these people need. You want him to forge a brilliant career? Well, he is. It may not be in a glamorous field but you'd better believe he's the best there is. Any father should be proud to call him his son.'

Charlie was speechless. So was Ignatius. They both stared at her. There was silence in the room for a few moments. Ignatius recovered first.

Ignoring Carrie, he said, 'We will talk about this at dinner on Sunday.'

'No, Father. We won't.'

Ignatius glared. 'You're refusing to come?'

'No. I'll be there all right. And so will Carrie and so will Dana. You get one chance, Father. One. If you so much as raise the subject of my career or Veronica, I will never come to dinner again. Ever. My days for tolerating your speeches, of keeping the peace, of taking the easy road are over.'

For a moment Ignatius turned redder and Carrie thought he was going to explode. But then she saw a light dawning. Ignatius was taking it in—the determination in his son's eyes, the firm grip Charlie had on her, their apparent solidarity. Her pulse hammered madly in her throat. Was Charlie just using her to get to his old man?

'Very well. Of course we would be delighted to have guests on Sunday.'

Carrie wasn't fooled. It was said too stiffly. But she was playing some bizarre part here where she hadn't been given the lines so she decided gracious acceptance was the way to go.

'Thank you, Dr Wentworth,' Carrie murmured.

Ignatius managed a sniff and a quick nod in Carrie's direction before turning on his heel and leaving the room.

It took a few seconds but then Carrie sagged against Charlie, the tension seeping out of her shoulders as the door shut. 'Well, that was—'

Charlie cut her off with a kiss. His lips were urgent and hard against her mouth and she opened up to him with greedy fervour. It had only been days but it had felt like a year. His kiss was hot and hungry and she grabbed hold of his shirt as her world shifted on its axis.

'God, I've missed you,' he muttered, pulling away to rain kisses on her face and down her neck.

'Oh, Charlie,' she whispered against his mouth, before he obliterated all words, all thoughts with another mind-scrambling kiss. She knew she shouldn't be complicating their separation any further, but it had been too long.

Charlie wanted to kiss her for ever. Go on for ever, but he knew there had to be words first. Talk first then kiss her. *Never stop kissing her.*

He pulled away reluctantly. 'I reckon, apart from me, you're the only person I've ever seen stand up to my old man like that.'

Carrie shrugged. 'He was belittling the man I loved.'

The words kind of tumbled out unchecked. And she didn't regret them. She had reacted to Ignatius Wentworth the same way she would have reacted to someone attacking Dana. Like a mother bear protecting her cub. She couldn't believe that Charlie's father was so blind.

'Love?' Charlie's world stopped. Surely she wouldn't jest about something this serious?

They looked at each other for a few moments. Carrie nodded. What the hell. It was out now. And she hadn't dropped dead or turned into a pillar of salt. If she was truly going to turn her back on this, she had to know how he felt for once and all.

'Thank God!' He drew her into a fierce hug. 'I love you, too.'

She pulled away, hardly able to believe her ears. Hardly daring to believe. She shook her head. After two years Rupert still hadn't loved her. 'You…you do? But this is so fast.'

He chuckled. Her whiskey gaze was muddy. Confused. And then he kissed her mouth and was gratified to feel her instant surrender, her pliant lips beneath his causing heat to pool in his groin.

'I've learnt the hard way that life's short and things can happen that you don't expect. Thanks to you, I made up my mind recently to start living my life again. And every cell in my body tells me that includes you.'

'What about Veronica?'

'I told you—Veronica is my past. I haven't loved her for a long time. I certainly never liked her very much. You're the woman for me. The only woman for me.'

'But your father…'

'My father may be a brilliant thoracic surgeon with an un-surpassed international reputation, but he's also a bigoted fool. If my father likes her so much, he can marry her. All I want is you. I promise you, Carrie, we'll never have to see my family, my father again. I'll never let him hurt you or Dana.'

And how would that make her feel? How could she ask that of him? To choose between his family and her? How long would their relationship last if she caused a rift between him and his family? Family was sacred—she only had to look around the centre to know that.

'I would never ask you to do that,' she said vehemently.

He shrugged, dropping his hands. 'I wouldn't worry. It's a fairly loose association as it is. I haven't felt like I belonged in my family for a long time. That's why I enjoyed spending time with you and Dana. You two are what a family should be. I want that for me. For us.'

Carrie looked up into his eyes, not daring to hope that things could be this perfect. 'Are you sure, Charlie? I know this has been a big problem for you.'

He nodded. 'I'm sure. Am I scared? Yes. Am I worried that I'll screw up? Yes. But every time I look into Dana's eyes there's this trust there. It's like she knows I can do it. You know? And, frankly, life without you, both of you, scares me more.'

Her hands crept up to cradle his face. His stubble grazed erotically against her palms. 'This is important, Charlie. Your father was right—you'll be taking on another man's child. Can you handle that?'

Charlie shook his head. On this he was definite. 'Dana's never been another man's child. She's been yours. She's one hundred per cent Douglas. And if you let me and you're willing to show me how to do it right, I'd like her to be mine also.'

Carrie nodded, tears blurring her eyes. 'Anything.'

Charlie smiled. 'Everything's going to be all right now. You, me and Dana. We're going to be all right now.'

Carrie swallowed the lump in her throat and blinked back tears. 'I love you, Charlie. Thank you. For everything.'

The words were bliss to his ears. Charlie knew that life was going to be perfect. 'I didn't do anything.'

'Oh, yes, you did. You gave me back my life. You helped me see the doctor inside that was dying to come out, and you gave Dana the one thing she wants most.'

He kissed her on the tip of her nose. 'A life supply of ding rolls?'

Carrie laughed. 'A daddy.'

Charlie kissed her full on the mouth. 'And you gave me a chance to be a father. A proper father. You gave me Dana. And the centre. That sounds like a fairly good trade to me.'

Carrie nodded, wrapping her arms around his neck. 'Should we shake on it?'

'I think we can do better than that. I think we should seal it with a kiss.'

Carrie smiled as his lips descended and hoped all their future agreements were sealed so delightfully.

EPILOGUE

'COME on, Grandpa Iggy.' Dana grabbed Ignatius Wentworth's hand and pulled insistently.

'Where are we going?' he grouched good-naturedly.

'Up the front,' Dana said, her voice leaving the eminent surgeon in no doubt who was in charge. 'Charlie's giving a speech.'

'Oh, right, then, lead the way.'

Carrie watched her daughter bring her grandfather closer to the front. She squeezed Charlie's hand. His entire family was sitting in the front row, looking expectantly at him. Dana had been determinedly bringing Ignatius and the rest of the Wentworths together for the last eighteen months. It had been gratifying, seeing the changes in his family and knowing that she and Dana had been responsible.

'Break a leg,' she whispered to her husband.

Charlie looked down into his wife's sexy gaze as he pulled at the uncomfortable tightness of his tie. 'I don't think you're supposed to say that to a doctor.'

Carrie smiled and straightened the tie for the third time. 'You'll be fine. You deserve this moment in the spotlight. This is your dream. Your vision.'

Charlie looked out over the crowd. It was an eclectic mix. Politicians rubbed shoulders with prostitutes. State government dignitaries sat alongside homeless kids. Police officers mixed with lawyers. Socialites circulated with journalists and missionaries.

And right in front was his family. Charlie still couldn't believe that in eighteen months a small child and a determined woman could have orchestrated such change. But they had. Carrie had been dogged, unwavering in her campaign to win his family over. To bring them all together as one.

Looking at his father now, he couldn't believe it was the same man he'd known for the last thirty-odd years. He was engrossed in conversation with a beribboned Dana, who was sitting on his lap, looking for all the world like she'd been a Wentworth from her conception. If Charlie hadn't seen the transformation with his own eyes, he'd have never believed it.

'I couldn't have done this without your help.' He glanced at Dana and his father. 'Any of it.'

'Your father's big fat cheque helped also.'

He chuckled. 'That's not what I meant.'

She winked. 'I know. Don't worry, I plan to hit you for a pay rise when I return to work after my maternity leave.'

He dropped a brief hard kiss on her lips as the director of the hospital board introduced him. His hand rested at her now non-existent waist and he could feel the swell of her belly where his baby grew larger every day. How could he have ever got this lucky?

Charlie took the podium to thunderous applause and a blast of wolf-whistles from the more colourful elements of the crowd.

'It is with great pleasure that I stand before you today at the opening of the new Valley Drop-In Centre. And may I say it's about time.'

Medical Romance™

COMING NEXT MONTH
TO MEDICAL ROMANCE SUBSCRIBERS

Visit www.eHarlequin.com for more details

Desert Doctor, Secret Sheikh by Meredith Webber

Dr. Jenny Stapleton has devoted herself to those in need around the globe, risking her life but never her heart. Then, in Zaheer, she meets Dr. Kam Rahman. But Kam is not just a doctor—he's a sheikh! Sheikh Kamid Rahman is soon to ascend the throne, and he wants this desert doctor as his queen!

A Single Dad at Heathermere by Abigail Gordon

The pretty village of Heathermere is not only a home but also a sanctuary for Jon Emmerson and his young daughter, Abby. Here he can simply focus on being a father and the local doctor, leaving his past far behind—until the day he bumps into childhood friend Dr. Laura Cavendish. Laura is a struggling single parent, too, and before long Jon realizes they are meant to be a family.

The Italian Count's Baby by Amy Andrews

Nurse Katya Petrov believes her unborn baby really needs its father. But talented Italian surgeon Count Benedetto, with whom she spent one passionate night, has no idea she is pregnant. Once he finds out, though, it becomes clear that he wants to be a father to his child, and he offers Katya marriage—for the baby's sake! But Katya secretly longs for Ben to one day give her his heart, as she has already given him hers.

The Heart Surgeon's Secret Son by Janice Lynn

Nurse Kimberly Brooks has postponed her week-long training session with leading heart surgeon Daniel Travis once already. Even though she feels like running for the hills, she can't put it off any longer. She has to go into surgery and face the man she once loved with all her heart. But, as the week goes on, Kimberly feels the pressure of her renewed feelings for Daniel, and of her untold secret—he is the father of her son.

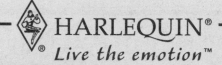

HARLEQUIN®
Live the emotion™

American ROMANCE®

Heart, Home & Happiness

HARLEQUIN®
Blaze™

Red-hot reads.

HARLEQUIN®

EVERLASTING LOVE™
Every great love has a story to tell™

 Harlequin® Historical
Historical Romantic Adventure!

HARLEQUIN®

HARLEQUIN ROMANCE®
From the Heart, For the Heart

HARLEQUIN®
INTRIGUE®
Breathtaking Romantic Suspense

Medical Romance™...
love is just a heartbeat away

 N^ext™

**There's the life you planned.
And there's what comes next.**

HARLEQUIN®
Presents
Seduction and Passion Guaranteed!

HARLEQUIN®
Super Romance®

Exciting, Emotional, Unexpected

Romantic
SUSPENSE

**Sparked by Danger,
Fueled by Passion.**

When Tech Sergeant Jacob "Mako" Stone opens
his door to a mysterious woman without a past,
he knows his time off is over. As threats to Dee's
life bring her and Jacob together, she must set
aside her pride and accept the help of the military
hero with too many secrets of his own.

Out of Uniform
by Catherine Mann

Available February wherever you buy books.

Silhouette® Desire

NEW YORK TIMES BESTSELLING AUTHOR

DIANA PALMER

A brand-new Long, Tall Texans novel

IRON COWBOY

*Available March 2008
wherever you buy books.*